What the press says about Harlequin Romances...

"...clean, wholesome fiction...always with an upbeat, happy ending."
— *San Francisco Chronicle*

"...a work of art."
— *The Globe & Mail*, Toronto

"Nothing quite like it has happened since *Gone With the Wind*..."
— *Los Angeles Times*

"...among the top ten..."
— *International Herald-Tribune*, Paris

"Women have come to trust these clean, easy-to-read love stories about contemporary people, set in exciting foreign places."
— *Best Sellers*, New York

OTHER

Harlequin Romances

by CHARLOTTE LAMB

Master of Comus

by

CHARLOTTE LAMB

Harlequin Books

TORONTO • LONDON • NEW YORK • AMSTERDAM • SYDNEY

Original hardcover edition published in 1978
by Mills & Boon Limited

ISBN 0-373-02181-X

Harlequin edition published July 1978

PRINTED IN U.S.A.

CHAPTER ONE

THEY travelled on the same flight to Athens. Leonie could see his smooth blond head from time to time when he turned to look out of the window. His hair and a tantalising portion of his profile; the long, classical nose, one insolent blue eye and the pale curve of his brow. She considered these thoughtfully, weighing them against what she knew of her cousin, Paul Caprel. Her knowledge of him was chiefly culled from newspaper gossip. His activities, both financial and amorous, were frequently plastered all over the popular papers. From an early age she had followed his adventures out of a secret admiration, regarding him rather in the light of a Byronic hero. He had been her chief claim to fame during her years at a monastic English girls' public school. After lights out, by the light of a romantic torch, she had read aloud his latest escapades to ecstatic murmurs of delight from her friends. She had kept a scrapbook of these clippings for years. Discreetly covered with brown paper and labelled 'My Family', it had escaped detection by the eagle-eyed schoolmistress who was in charge of her house. Leonie read it in the privacy of a steamy bathroom, perched on the side of the bath while she gazed at Paul's wild, handsome, disreputable features, and sighed out her undying love.

After leaving school she had refused the chance of a university education, in preference choosing a London art school, where she met a large body of wild, disreputable young men and rapidly abandoned the remote dream for the reality. Her college years had been fun. She had felt as if she was breaking out of prison after the nun-like years at her school. Her guardian, a busy middle-aged aunt who lived in Bath and bred poodles, thoroughly disapproved of Leonie's decision to take up art as a career, but accepted it since the girl was by then eighteen and legally of age.

Leonie's father had been a quiet country solicitor until the day when he met her mother, the slim, dark, exquisite granddaughter of a Greek millionaire. She had whirled him away into a strangely different world from any he had ever known. Her parents were separated and indifferent, and only her grandfather had registered a protest at her marriage to a thirty-year-old solicitor with a small practice and no fortune. Elektra Caprel had shrugged her slender shoulders, laughed and married her sensible Englishman. A year later Leonie had been born. When she was three her parents were killed in an air crash and her father's sister became her guardian. Elektra's grandfather, Argon Caprel, had sent emissaries to demand her custody, but they had come up against the rock of Aunt Mary's tenacity. Aunt Mary had not liked Elektra Caprel, nor had she approved of her brother's marriage. It had been too far out of their sphere of life, but her strong sense of family duty had impelled her to bring Leonie up properly. She could not permit her brother's child to be whisked away to Greece. Argon Caprel had threatened from his remote eyrie on a Greek island —either Leonie was given up to him or he would cut her out of his will. Aunt Mary had been indifferent, indeed, she suspected and distrusted the idea of such a large fortune. Leonie would be better off without it.

So, brought up on notions of duty and common sense, nourished on bread and butter pudding and lamb chops, Leonie had grown up with just the appearance and manners her aunt desired of her. Cool, courteous, very English, she played tennis in summer and hockey in winter, wore well-tailored clothes and understated make-up, liked the theatre and the opera but disliked ballet, and had a circle of friends very much like herself. Her three years at art school had broadened her view of life considerably. For a while she had worn jeans and kaftans, let her dark hair hang in wild curls, stayed up all night for parties. But Aunt Mary had done her work too well. After this initial outburst of freedom, Leonie had settled down into a compromise between her staid background and her artistic surroundings.

She had made a large number of friends at college. When she left after three years she got a job with an advertising agency on a bright young team working for a range of popular products. The work was highly paid, stimulating and challenging. She had a flat in Chelsea a few minutes' walk away from the river, a small white car and a busy social life.

One night at a party she met a man whose face

was instantly recognisable—a racing driver with a sallow skin, curly black hair and an engaging grin. Leo Ashenden dated her within a week of their first meeting, and went on seeing her whenever he was in England for the next three months. When he proposed marriage she was both enchanted and astonished—so astonished that she did not speak for several moments, and Leo, peering down at her face, said with his grin, 'Does silence mean yes or no?' It had meant yes.

It had never occurred to her to tell him of her connection with the Caprel family. Her great-grandfather had made no attempt to get in touch with her since his rebuff eighteen years earlier. When Leo casually asked her if she had told Argon Caprel of their engagement, she had been surprised. 'No, why should I?' Innocently, she had explained that her great-grandfather had cut her out of his will and took no interest in her, and that she, for her part, was indifferent to him. Leo had listened with an odd expression. Only weeks later did Leonie comprehend. Realisation came with a curt letter from him informing her of his engagement to the daughter of a South African copper baron. He had expressed cool regret, adding that he had decided that they were not compatible. Leonie's heart had winced, but her head had rapidly come to the conclusion that Leo had only been interested in her as her great-grandfather's heiress. At what point he had discovered the family connection she would never know, but she suspected it to have been early on in their relationship.

By a strange coincidence, a week later she received a letter from her great-grandfather himself, inviting her to visit him on his Greek island.

It would be a family party, he told her. He was now seventy and in poor health. He did not expect to live long, and he wanted to see her before he died.

Leonie had consulted Aunt Mary. Reading the letter with a wry expression, her aunt advised her to go. 'It's your duty. He is your great-grandfather, after all. But it must be your own decision. You're an adult now.'

So Leonie had written to accept. The following day a London branch of the Caprel organisation rang her to say that her ticket to Athens had been booked, that she would be met at Athens and flown by private plane to the island of Comus. She had said nothing to the woman who spoke to her, but her spirit of independence had prickled angrily, and she had written to her great-grandfather to protest at his high-handed behaviour.

'I can certainly afford to pay my own fare and will refund you the cost of my ticket,' she had written. Argon Caprel had replied via his secretary with a cold letter telling her that since he had requested her presence he would be responsible for her travel arrangements. Leonie had written back curtly saying that no one but herself could be responsible for her and enclosing the cheque for a first-class fare to Athens. Argon wrote to her himself a few days later. The letter was brief and consisted of three words: Damn your impudence. Clipped to the letter was a receipt for her cheque. She had studied the heavy black scrawl with interest and amusement. For the first time she felt curiosity about Argon.

Now, on the flight, she saw her cousin Paul seated a few rows ahead of her, and wondered if he, too, were bound for Comus. He was her great-grand-father's heir—everyone knew that. He was a jet-setter, flying constantly between London, Paris, New York and Athens. Thirty years old, in charge of his own fast-growing property company, he was a notor-ious international playboy with a penchant for svelte young women and fast cars. He had never married, but engagements had been hinted at from time to time, and his extra-marital gaiety had kept the gossip columnists happy for years.

As he walked back along the deck their eyes met once, and Leonie saw by his blank expression that he did not know her. There was no reason why he should. She was the alienated member of the family. She had the advantage of him since she knew a great deal about him, while Paul knew nothing about her.

When they left the plane at Athens the heat struck her like a blowtorch, setting up a pounding in her temples and blinding her eyes. She made her way to the reception area and gave her name to the desk clerk, as she had been instructed. A few moments later a small, dark Greek materialised courteously, took charge of her luggage and escorted her back across the tarmac to a smaller plane waiting in the full blaze of the sun.

When she climbed aboard she found herself faced with Paul once more. He was lounging back in a well-upholstered chair, a glass in his hand. Through elegant sun-glasses he scrutinised her curiously. Her guide bowed to him. 'Miss Leonie,' he said in softly accented English.

Above the sunglasses Paul's pale brows rose to a perfect arch. 'Good lord! The dark horse!'

Leonie felt herself flushing angrily at the mockery in his tone. She nodded to him and sat down in the seat beside him, occupying herself with her seat belt and a handful of magazines. A few moments later the plane took off into the bright Greek sky.

Paul turned his head to study her coolly. 'So you're making an appearance at last!'

She saw no point in replying to that beyond a small, polite nod. Accepting a glass of orange flavoured with gin, she leaned back and pretended to study the horizon. When the plane dipped down she caught a strange, slanting glimpse of the Aegean sea below them, dark blue and sun-dappled. Here and there the blue was interrupted by an island, jutting up out of the waves, grey and shadowed, a rocky explosion from the surrounding sea.

'You live in England, I gather,' Paul drawled, his insolent gaze still fixed on her.

She started. He had been silent so long she had forgotten his presence in her fascination with the view below them. She turned, eyes widening. 'Yes.'

He took off his sunglasses and the blue eyes flashed into view, taking her breath away by their brightness and beauty. He really was an incredibly handsome young man. 'So you speak!' The tone was lightly mocking. 'I was beginning to suspect you were dumb.'

She shrugged. 'I have no gift for small talk with strangers.'

His mouth curved in a hard smile. 'You mean you share Argon's arrogant disregard of the conventions. And you're proud of it.'

The comparison did not please her. She frowned. 'Not at all. I meant precisely what I said. When I have nothing to say I say nothing. It saves a great deal of wasted time.'

He threw back his head and laughed. His skin had a golden tan which intensified the blond of his smooth hair and gave to his blue eyes an almost dazzling brilliance.

'My God, but you're a Caprel all right! A pity you weren't a boy—Argon would have been delighted with you.'

She finished her drink and leaned back again, lowering her lids against the brightness of the sun flooding through the window. They were flying lower now. Were they coming in to land? she wondered.

Paul spoke again, close beside her ear. 'Do you know what to expect when we reach Comus? You know about the villa?'

She shook her head. 'I know nothing about my mother's family except what I read in the newspapers.' On the last words she gave him a cool, measuring glance.

He met it thoughtfully. 'Ah, the newspapers! That's a shot at me, I take it? You've heard about my scandalous goings-on and you disapprove, in that cold English fashion?' He leaned closer, lowering his voice intimately. 'Does the prospect of spending a few weeks at Comus with such a wild young man terrify you?'

'Don't be ludicrous,' she said calmly. Her golden-brown eyes gazed at him with unflattering contempt. 'I'm not a child to be frightened of bogeymen. Your private life is your own affair. It doesn't interest me.' She felt a slight qualm of conscience, remembering her long-forgotten schooldays and her nights of romantic contemplation of Paul's photographs in the newspaper. When she was fourteen the twenty-one-year-old playboy had seemed a man of the world. Seven years later the gap between them had considerably diminished, although she had to admit that she had spent her first twenty-one years in a far more circumspect fashion.

Their eyes clashed. Unknowingly, her brown eyes offered him a defiant challenge. His blue ones narrowed, reading the expression, and a curious look came into his handsome face.

At thirty Paul Caprel was hopelessly spoilt; born with a silver spoon in his mouth and a flotilla of adoring young women to pursue him ceaselessly. Pleasure had occupied his leisure time and spilt over into his working hours. He had a good mind, quick and clever, but had never acquired the habit of concentration which accompanies money-making. The constant company of beautiful and available young women had left him a low opinion of the opposite sex. From them he expected nothing but amusement.

The thought of marriage had never entered his head; there was no need to bother.

At times, in the intervals of a life devoted to restless pleasure, he had felt vaguely discontented with his world. Surely there ought to be something more than this? he had sometimes asked himself. But these moments of melancholy reflection had never lasted long. Another lovely girl would swim over the horizon and he would settle down to the pursuit, only to find his rapid victory dull once achieved. His looks, his charm, his glamour and above all his money ensured swift conquest, but Paul always found the affair boring after a time.

For some time now he had felt restlessly discontented, but he did not know what it was he wanted, only that nothing his money could buy him could satisfy his hunger for permanence, for stability, for happiness.

The plane was definitely circling an island now. Leonie gazed down eagerly at rough-hewn hills covered with a green haze of bushes and scrub, beaches of silver and curling white-topped waves of a blue which reminded her of Paul's eyes.

'Fasten your seat belt,' Paul reminded her.

She glanced at him, her eyes dazed, and he sighed and leaned over to fasten the belt for her. At that moment she moved, too, and their hands touched. Leonie felt a queer shiver run down her spine and her breathing tightened. Paul clipped the belt with a metallic snap, withdrew his hands and leaned back.

The plane came into land. Leonie watched the blue waters skim past. They were landing on the beach, she realised. There was a slight bump and they were stationary. Paul stood up with leisurely grace, bending his head to avoid banging it on the rack above. Leonie stood up, too, dropping her magazines, and Paul knelt to pick them up. She took them from him nervously, feeling oddly awkward and ungainly.

Something had happened when his hands touched hers, though she was not sure what. She only knew that something had flashed between them, in silent semaphore; an emotion, a challenge, a change in their attitudes. She felt a heightened awareness of him as she left the plane. He went first and helped her down the steps. As she stood beside him, her head reached his shoulder, although she had always thought of herself as quite a tall girl. He must be just over six foot, she decided. His lean build was deceptive. In photographs he looked shorter.

A silvery limousine waited to drive them to the villa. Argon owned the whole island, Paul explained. He had built himself a palace of a house in a remote fastness in the hills. All the other houses on the island were occupied either by people who worked for him at the villa, or by farmers and shepherds who worked on the land. Argon never left Comus now. He was not happy away from his home. His companies were run by employees who reported to him daily on the telephone and by letter. He still kept a finger in every pie, but he did it from his remote island kingdom.

'He's very frail,' Paul added gently.

Leonie glanced at his golden profile. 'You're fond of him,' she stated.

He looked at her with faint hauteur. 'Of course.' She saw that he disliked such private emotions being discussed. So something, at least, was sacred to him!

'Who else will be there?' she asked. 'Tell me about the family.'

He frowned. 'The family? There's no one else, just Argon. And myself, of course.' The blue eyes slid over her. 'And now you, my dear cousin.'

She was taken aback. 'I had imagined there would be several of my aunts...'

He lifted a careless shoulder in an elegant shrug. 'Aunt Alexa never leaves her village on Capri and Aunt Athene died last year. Neither of them had children, as you probably know. We're not a very productive lot, we Caprels.'

The limousine swept up a smooth tarmac road. Behind a group of trees the house flashed into sight: a long, white villa with green shutters and a flowery creeper spilling along the lower walls. Silk-smooth emerald lawns surrounded it, and beds of gay flowers and shrubs gave it a colourful setting. To the left behind it Leonie caught a glimpse of a swimming pool with a brightly tiled surround. Striped umbrellas gave some shade to the white tables and chairs which stood around the pool.

'It looks like a holiday camp,' she said involuntarily.

Paul laughed shortly. 'For God's sake don't tell Argon your opinion. He wouldn't be amused.'

Neither, she realised, was he, despite his laughter. The blue eyes were hard beneath their pale brows. Paul was, in fact, feeling a rising irritation. He had an affection for Comus which he did not feel for any other place on earth, and this girl's refusal to be impressed annoyed him.

The car pulled up in front of a shady verandah. Grapes grew along the slatted roof, hanging down in green clusters almost in reach of her hand. An old woman in a black dress hobbled out, leaning on a stick, and gave a cry of welcome in Greek. Paul moved quickly towards her and was embraced, kissed on both cheeks, held away so that the tired old blue eyes could study him.

Paul smiled patiently under this, saying something which brought a quick smile to the old woman's wrinkled face. Then he turned and indicated Leonie.

The old woman gave a little cry of obvious pleasure and spoke. Leonie smiled, looked at Paul. 'I don't speak Greek.'

The old woman looked horrified, clearly understanding her. She spoke then in English with a thick Greek accent. 'You do not speak Greek? Ah, how terrible! A Caprel not to speak Greek!'

Paul's insolent gaze made Leonie angry. 'This is an English Caprel,' he drawled. 'Quite a different breed, you will find, but a Caprel, nonetheless, Clyte.'

Clyte was staring openly, her blue eyes taking in every part of Leonie's appearance. 'Yes,' she said at last, 'you are right, Paul. A Caprel—one of the black Caprels.' She smiled at Leonie. 'There are two strains in the family, you know. Some are black-haired, others fair. Your grandfather was dark. You have inherited his colouring. Paul's grandfather was fair.'

Leonie smiled her interest. The old woman spoke quickly in Greek again and Paul laughed.

'Yes, she has the gift of silence, Clyte. She tells me she never speaks if she has nothing to say.' His lifted eyebrows mocked Leonie gently. 'A rare gift in women.'

'Come quickly now to Argon,' the old woman said, taking Leonie's hand. 'He has been waiting impatiently to see you.' She gave her a sly grin. 'You angered him by your letters, but you gave him a great desire to see you.'

'Quarrelling with him already?' Paul asked.

'She returned the money he had paid for her fare here,' Clyte told him, chuckling. 'I have not seen him so excited for a long time. I thought he would have a stroke. But excitement is good for him. It stirs up his blood. She did him good.'

Paul's glance measured Leonie once more. 'Pride and arrogance,' he said thoughtfully. 'Oh, a Caprel to your fingertips, my dear.'

She burned with anger but did not retort. Clyte, grinning, led the way into the cool interior of the villa. The magnificence of the furnishings took Leonie's breath away. She had never seen such superb decor. The long saloon they entered was marble-floored, pale blue and white, with Greek legends illustrated in mosaic circles here and there. Paintings hung on the walls, and she recognised the

styles of some of the greater modern artists, including several early Picasso sketches framed in
black wood. The furniture was of the French empire
period; ornate, delicate, highly polished. Flowers
stood everywhere, their colour giving warmth to the
room. The deep-buttoned silken chaise-longue was
scattered with matching cushions.

Clyte hobbled past all this without a glance,
taking it for granted. Paul watched Leonie's expres-
sive face closely. He wanted her to feel the charm of
Comus.

They walked through a marble-floored hall and
up a flight of wide, sunlit stairs. Argon Caprel's
bedroom was the master suite at the front of the
house, facing the broad curve of the blue sea.

Clyte knocked on the closed door, and a deep
voice bade them enter. Leonie's swift glance took in
the whole room; deep-piled white carpet, silk lamps,
fitted wardrobes and dressing-table, a cushioned
bedroom chair and the bed which dominated the
room.

Seated upright against a heap of pillows was a
broad-shouldered old man with white hair and a
massive, rock-like countenance from which shone
eyes of her own golden brown.

They stared at each other for a long, silent moment. Then Argon Caprel said in his deep voice,
'So! You are the English girl.'

'I am Leonie Wilde,' she countered. 'How are
you, Great-grandfather?'

'Stand by the window,' he replied obliquely. 'I
want to see you better.'

She stiffened, but obeyed. Three pairs of eyes watched her remorselessly. Rigid-backed, she lifted her chin defiantly, she stared back at them.

'You're your mother's child,' Argon said at last.

'A Caprel,' nodded Clyte, with satisfaction.

Argon flashed her a curious glance, as if asking a question, and Clyte nodded to him again, as if agreeing with an unspoken remark.

'Do you enjoy your job?' Argon asked abruptly.

Leonie was surprised that he knew about it, but nodded. 'Very much. It's exciting work.'

'You are good at it?'

She smiled, her teeth very even and white. 'I think so. I'm very highly paid.'

'You can paint while you are here,' he told her. 'Comus is an artist's paradise.'

She glanced out of the window at the hillside which fell away steeply to a shelving beach. 'Yes, I should say it was!'

'I am tired,' he said suddenly, relaxing against his pillows. 'Come and see me again tomorrow and tell me more about yourself. Paul will look after you tonight.'

She saw that he did, indeed, look pale, and she threw a look of anxious enquiry to Paul, who smiled reassuringly, taking her by the arm to lead her out of the room.

'Goodnight, Great-grandfather,' she said over her shoulder.

'Goodnight, Leonie,' he replied. 'I am sorry our first meeting is so short, but we will make up for it tomorrow.'

Paul waited on the landing for Clyte to re-emerge, and asked her to show Leonie to her room. Clyte led her to a large room at the back of the house looking on to the garden. It was as elegantly furnished as the rest of the house; ultra-comfortable with every modern convenience, including a shower cubicle and a television.

'Not,' said Paul later, 'that you can get much on the things. The transmitter only just reaches here. In calm weather one can get a good picture, but during a storm all you get is a blizzard of white dots.'

'I doubt if I shall want to watch it, anyway,' she said. 'I shan't be here long enough to exhaust the pleasures of sightseeing.'

He surveyed her insolently. 'I'd forgotten you were an artist. That explains a great deal.'

She knew she would regret asking, but she did ask. 'What does it explain?'

'Your self-assurance and hard opinions,' he drawled. 'Artists always have a high opinion of themselves and a low one of others.'

'I find such generalisations worthless,' she said crisply, determined not to be affected by the charming picture he made, lounging against the cocktail cabinet with a glass in his hand and his golden head honey-smooth in the lamplight.

The blue eyes brightened. 'I get the impression you think us all worthless: Argon, the villa and myself.' His smile taunted her. 'Isn't that so?'

'I have no idea of my great-grandfather yet. As for yourself ... well,' she shrugged, 'if the cap fits!'

'Tart as a lemon, aren't you?' he asked with amusement.

'You shouldn't ask for my opinion if you only want polite lies,' she said sturdily.

'Your opinion?' He straightened up, his eyes blazingly angry suddenly. 'Your opinion isn't worth a straw since you came here determined to despise the lot of us, determined to see nothing admirable or interesting on Comus. Your mind is like concrete. Nothing permeates it. You're a narrow-minded, bigoted little beast!'

Leonie felt a pricking of tears at the iciness of his tone. Honesty compelled her to admit the truth of much of what he had said, yet his frank condemnation still hurt.

'I'm an outsider here,' she flung back recklessly. 'For eighteen years my great-grandfather ignored my existence. Do you really expect me to be floored by all the evidences of his wealth and power, or, for that matter, by your famous charm and good looks? I may be prejudiced, but that's hardly surprising considering the circumstances!'

He put down his glass and came towards her, and she looked at him in alarm. His tone silky-smooth, he murmured, 'So my famous charm and good looks leave you cold, do they, dear cousin? I wonder...'

She involuntarily stepped back, frightened as much by the unaccustomed pounding of her own pulses as by the expression of intent menace on his face.

Paul caught her by the elbows and held her at arms' length, staring down with an odd expression at

her uplifted features, their fine-boned strength soft-
ened by the lamplight into a sort of beauty. 'Your
eyes are like pansies,' he whispered softly. 'They
have little golden centres. A pity they are so cold.'

'Don't waste your charm on me,' she snapped,
'I'm immune.'

He laughed at that, the insolent blue eyes caressing her face. 'Are you sure? Why is that pulse beating at the base of your throat, then? Why are your
fingers trembling as I hold you?'

'Let me go, damn you,' she whispered huskily.
'This phoney love talk of yours makes me want to
throw up!'

He laughed again, but harshly, and released her,
although he continued to watch her closely. 'You
have a nasty tongue, my love. So tell me—what
makes you think you're immune? Another man? It
usually is. What's he like, this Romeo of yours?'

'Oh, you'd get on famously together,' she snapped. 'You have so much in common—glib tongues,
a fast line in cheap patter and not a shred of genuine
feeling in your souls.'

'Ouch!' His blue eyes narrowed. 'I gather the
gentleman left you somewhat disillusioned.'

'He left me for an heiress,' she informed him bitterly. 'To do him credit, the experience probably did
me good. I learnt a lot from him.'

'None of it very pleasant, apparently.'

Her lip curled. 'Education often proves unpleas-
ant.'

'You loved him?' The question shot at her abruptly.

Her brown eyes shifted, then the thick black lashes descended to veil her expression. 'You ask too many questions.'

'My dear, it's obvious,' he drawled. 'Such bitterness could only have been bred by love. Well, you're well rid of him, if that's any comfort to you. I can't say I'm flattered by the comparison, however. To my knowledge I've never hunted heiresses.'

'You don't need to,' she retorted. 'You use the same techniques for different purposes.'

He put out a long finger to touch her cheek, and her skin tightened under the touch. 'Poor little thing! You've been through the fire, haven't you? Unlucky all round—with your family first, then your love affair. No wonder you're as stony as that hillside out there.'

She found his gentleness too weakening. Moving away, she turned her back on him to stare out of the window at the dark night sky. 'I'm tired. I think I'll go to bed,' she said.

'I'm astonished,' he said. 'I hadn't thought you were a coward.'

She turned angrily, met his amused gaze and was forced to laugh. 'No, really. I'm exhausted.'

The blue eyes laughed. 'I believe you, despite appearances. Sleep well.'

Leonie went upstairs to her own room and stood in the darkness for a moment waiting for her heart to calm down. At a distance Paul Caprel had had a romantic glamour which was enthralling. She found his actual presence far more potent. Common sense, so long instilled, so much part of her nature now, warned against taking any part of his charm seriously. It was second nature to the man to flirt with every available female. He was another Leo, as she had told him, smooth-tongued and plausible, yet basically not to be trusted.

'I'll never fall in love like that again,' she told the warm, scented night, and wished she believed her words herself.

CHAPTER TWO

DAWN conferred a cool sweetness on the island air. Under the pines which shaded the beach path a small grey lizard scuttled in search of flies, and the sea thistles were alive with gaudy butterflies, with long forked tails, flicking to and fro with easy grace.

Leonie had awoken at first light and gone downstairs to find the servants moving about quietly on sandalled feet. Her appearance created something of a stir, but Clyte was sent for, and persuaded her to sit down in the breakfast room and eat some rolls and fruit with a pot of strong coffee.

Still not certain as to Clyte's actual role in the household, although convinced of her importance to Argon, Leonie enquired as to the possibilities of swimming on the beach. Clyte smiled, her gold-filled teeth glinting against her pale gums.

'Of course, my dear, of course you may swim. You have brought a costume?'

Leonie nodded. 'I hoped I would get a chance to sunbathe.'

Clyte's pale old eyes surveyed her. 'You have a good skin for taking the sun. A Greek colouring.'

After breakfast, Leonie went up to her room to fetch a large towel and swimming costume, then found her way down the beach path with Clyte's directions as a guide. The way was stony and difficult, but at last she emerged on the beach; changed behind a large rock and ran down into the tantalising coolness of the water.

She swam like a fish, diving under the blue swell of the waves now and then, or floating and staring up at the concealing canopy of the sky. As the sun climbed the skies the refreshing coolness left the beach and it grew hotter. She spread her towel on the sand and lay down on her stomach. After a while she anointed herself with sun-tan lotion and turned over on to her back. The heat of the sun made her drowsy. Her lids flickered and closed.

She did not hear the soft grate of sandals on sand until Paul spoke to her.

'You must be careful, you know. This sun is deceptive. You don't want sunstroke.'

She reluctantly opened her eyes. He stood over her, very tall and long-limbed, in dark swim trunks, a towel over one arm. His tanned face wore a sardonic mask as he contemplated her long, slender half-naked body, travelling openly over the pointed swell of her breasts, her flat stomach and slim thighs.

Flushing, she sat up and drew her knees up to her chin as if to hide herself.

He crouched beside her and picked up the bottle of lotion. 'I'll put some of this on your back. Time you turned over.'

She was too late to protest. He had tipped some into his palm and began to smooth it over her back. His long fingers stroked caressingly down her shoulders, following the faint golden line of down along her back to the swell of her hips. He took his time, arousing pulses in places she had not suspected of possessing them.

'That's enough,' she exclaimed abruptly. 'Thank you.'

His hand halted, spread out against her skin, the long fingers splayed in a caress. 'Did you sleep well?' he asked without removing his hand.

'Yes, thank you.' She moved restlessly. 'I'll lie down again now. Are you going to swim?'

He withdrew his hand. 'Yes,' he agreed. He dropped his towel beside hers and sprinted down the beach into the water. Leonie watched as his lean body hit the waves and dived into them. He was more muscled, more athletic than she had expected, his body strongly shaped and lean. I must be careful, she told herself. He's far too attractive. She lay down on her stomach, exposing her back to the relentless sun.

A short while later a towel dropped across her body and Paul flung himself down beside her. 'You must cover up now. Too much sun too soon is dangerous.'

The sun isn't the only thing around here that's dangerous, she thought wryly. She turned her head, her wet hair flicking him across the face, and found him far too close for comfort.

The bright blue eyes mocked her. 'Clyte told me you were down here. An early riser, I gather. How very English!'

'Is Clyte one of the family or a servant?' she asked him, avoiding more personal subjects.

'Neither,' he said briskly, with a hard look. 'She

has worked for Argon since she was fourteen years old, but she's far more than a servant, if less than family.' He grinned. 'I suspect they were more than master and servant when they were young, to be honest.'

She felt vaguely shocked, and her expression betrayed the feeling. Paul gave her a sardonic look. 'They're old now, but they had their moments, no doubt. Why should that shock you? They're human beings with ordinary human emotions and human needs.'

Leonie built a tiny wall of sand with her fingers, embedding shells and pieces of wet seaweed in it. Paul lay and watched her, his head cradled on his folded arms. She has a dark, passionate face, he thought, but the passion has been forced down, if not out of sight, and that damned English education of hers has erected a glass wall around her. She was like a sleeping princess in a crystal cavern, and the sight of her created in him a savage desire to hack his way through the ice with brutal disregard for any emotional damage he might do. It would have been better for her, with her hereditary instincts, to be brought up by Argon as a Greek. The lines of that face were all Greek; stormy, dark with the austere bone structure of an island people accustomed to a hard existence.

At first sight he had been deceived by the cool hauteur of her English mask. Now he saw through the mask to the Greek soul within it.

Her wall crumbled suddenly. He laughed. 'A

pointless pastime, building with sand. Time you learnt that.'

She sat up, flicking sand from her fingers. 'I think I'll go back to the house. Argon may be ready to see me.'

Paul rolled over on to his back and surveyed her insolently, a hand shading his eyes from the sun. 'Get dressed first, then. Argon has a very old-fashioned attitude to women. He expects them to be fully clothed.'

'I was not intending to march into his bedroom like this,' she retorted.

'You never know with the English.'

'Chauvinist!'

He laughed. 'Proud of it, too.'

Her dark face lit with an answering smile. 'Yes,' she said. 'I can understand that.'

Paul's eyes narrowed. A gleam shot into them, the sudden delight of the collector who sees a rare object he has long desired. 'You're half Greek yourself, remember.'

She looked vaguely at a loss. 'I'm just beginning to realise it.'

'Had you never realised it before?'

She shook her head. 'Not really.'

'But you knew!'

She shrugged. 'Knowing a fact is a very different thing from feeling it in your bones. My mind knew that I had Greek blood, but my heart had never felt it. It was not until I actually got here that I began to feel in any way Greek.' She frowned. 'It began when I looked down from the plane and saw the Aegean, I think. Then when I met Argon...' Her voice broke off and she smiled. 'Blood is thicker than water, we say in England.'

'Ah, but to a Greek the saying has more meaning. The Greek family is a much stronger unit, more cohesive, more powerful. Family loyalties are sacrosanct here.'

'That was not my mother's experience,' she pointed out.

Paul grimaced. 'She broke a tribal law. She married without the consent of the family.'

'And became a family outlaw!'

'All law can be savage,' he said.

'How easily you say that! How smug and narrow-minded you can be, Paul Caprel.'

He surveyed her through his pale lashes. 'Your aunt refused to let you come to Comus. She was just as ruthless as Argon.'

'At any time in the last eighteen years Argon could have visited England. My aunt wouldn't have refused to let him see me. She's a strong-minded lady, but she's fair. When I agreed to come here it was on her advice.'

'Perhaps she felt she had cheated you of your inheritance,' Paul said coolly. 'You were cut out of Argon's will because she refused to send you here, you know.'

'You don't know my aunt or you wouldn't imagine that money has any significance for her. She brought me up to be independent and earn my own living. She has no time for rich and idle people.'

He grinned. 'Like me?'

Her brown eyes answered silently. She turned and walked away up the stony path. He watched her with an abstracted expression. Her back was elegantly straight, her carriage graceful, the black hair dried by the sun and flying loosely as she moved. Paul rolled over and picked up a handful of sand, letting it trickle through his long fingers. The blue eyes were serious as he watched the silvery sand sift downwards in a fine shower.

In her room Leonie changed into a simple, sleeveless peach-coloured linen dress. Clyte had told her that Argon had breakfasted and was eager to see her. Brushing her hair, she studied herself in the mirror, then swept up the black locks into a neat, classical chignon and pinned them securely. The hairstyle restored her usual image. On the beach she had felt herself changing in some way, her emotions fluid and disturbed. She needed to establish a base from which to explore these changes without committing herself. How much Paul had to do with her new attitudes she was not sure. That he had already begun to affect her deeply she was forced to admit, and the realisation worried her. She had enough emotional problems coping with the discovery of her Greek roots. She did not want a further complication in the shape of a man.

Argon welcomed her eagerly, his brown face split with a wide smile.

Instinctively Leonie bent and kissed his cheek. He put up a gnarled hand to catch her fingers and pressed them.

She sat down beside the bed on a comfortable, silk

upholstered chair and smiled at him.

'So. You are settling in?' he asked.

'Yes. My room is delightful, thank you.'

He brushed the thanks away with a graceful gesture. 'Clyte tells me you have been on the beach with Paul this morning.'

'Yes. I swam and sunbathed.'

His brown eyes watched her with curious attention. 'And what is your opinion of Paul?'

She hesitated, then shrugged. 'I'm afraid we rub each other up the wrong way.'

His eyes brightened. 'Ah? There have been clashes?'

'Shall we say we exist in a state of armed neutrality?' she put it lightly.

He nodded. 'That is good.'

Leonie was taken aback. 'Good?'

'But of course. Between a man and a woman there can only be one relationship—the sexual one. What people call the platonic friendship is only another name for indifference. Had you and Paul become friends it would have meant that you did not find each other attractive.'

She felt her cheeks burn. 'I thought I explained. I don't find Paul attractive. If anything, I dislike him...'

The door behind her opened and Paul himself came into the room. Leonie swung round, startled, and their eyes met. Paul bowed mockingly.

'Please, don't mind me, dear cousin. Do go on. I am riveted.'

She turned back to Argon, her back rigid with

irritation. Argon chuckled, looking from one to the other of them. 'I am glad you have joined us, Paul. I have something to say to you both. Sit down beside Leonie.'

Paul drew up a chair and lounged back in it, his long legs thrust out. Beneath his lashes he glanced at Leonie, approvingly inspecting her dress and hair. It did not escape his attention that she had restored herself to her original English look, and the fact amused him.

'Leonie, when your aunt refused to let you come to Greece, I warned her that I would cut you out of my will, and I am a man of my word. By the will of God, Paul has proved to be my only male heir, and so for some years my will has made him my chief heir, as he knows. Indeed, as the world knows.' Argon looked directly at Paul. 'I left you free to choose your own path, Paul. I am going to speak freely in front of Leonie, since she is one of the family. I have not been pleased with your manner of life. You spend too much time in idle pleasure. Your business has been neglected in consequence, and judging by past experience, if I left you the lion's share of my holdings you would fritter a large part of my fortune away on your pursuit of pleasure.'

Paul was sitting upright now, his brows drawn together in a straight line. The blue eyes had lost their smile. The mouth had straightened and the chin was clenched.

'I will not argue with all that,' he said coldly. 'I do, however, dispute your right to haul me over the coals in front of a girl we neither of us knew a week ago.'

'I chose to speak in front of Leonie for a reason,' Argon said harshly. 'Bearing in mind your past record, I have decided, having now met Leonie and seen what sort of girl she is, to leave everything to her.'

Paul made no sound. Leonie, totally astounded, made a movement of angry protest. 'No!' She stared at her great-grandfather. 'You can't do that! That isn't fair. You've promised Paul all these years..

Paul interrupted her fiercely. 'Please! I can fight my own battles. I don't need a woman to do it for me. My great-grandfather has the right to dispose of his property as he sees fit. I don't need his money. My company has not gone bankrupt, even though he is right when he says it has not been too successful. I can manage to survive with what I have now.'

'But I don't want the beastly money!' She glared at him, her face now reflecting all the passionate nature he had suspected.

He shrugged. 'That is beside the point. You have as much right to it as I have. The people who run the companies now will go on doing so for ever. You will only need to sit tight and let the money accumulate.'

Leonie looked at Argon. 'I'm sorry. I appreciate the gesture, but I truly do not want you to do this. I would hate it.'

He smiled at her. 'You have a good heart, but Paul has had his chance to prove himself, and has failed. I could not allow the family fortune to be squandered on his pleasure. Having met you, I am sure you would be far more careful with my money.'

'I'm sure Paul will change when...' she began.

'He is thirty, not a boy,' Argon broke in flatly. 'I, too, thought that he would change, settle down, become more responsible. But the years have passed and Paul goes on in the same way. All he cares for is pleasure.'

Paul stood up. 'I accept your decision, Argon. I'll leave you to talk to Leonie alone.'

'No,' she protested, rising, too. 'Argon, please, don't do this...'

'There is another way,' Argon said softly.

She turned to look down at him hopefully. 'Yes?'

Paul waited, too, his hand on the door. Argon looked from one to the other, his eyes watchful.

'Marriage,' he said.

The word dropped into a silence which lengthened. Then Paul wrenched open the door and went out of the room like a charging lion. Argon called him back in a sharp, angry voice, and Paul stopped dead, his back to them.

Leonie was scarlet with mortification and anger. Before she could speak Argon went on quickly. 'By a marriage between the two of you I could provide for your future and be sure that the Caprel fortune would be secure. You are not so close in blood that it should matter—you are only second cousins. Paul has shown no signs of choosing a wife for himself, and you, Leonie, have no husband in mind. I realise that arranged marriages are a thing of the past, but I am sure you will both realise how sensible this arrangement would be.'

'Sensible!' Paul's voice was smothered, hot with rage. He still stood with his back to them so that Leonie could not see his face.

'All I ask is that you consider the idea,' Argon said gently. 'Take your time. But remember, I am very old, and I may not live much longer. I want to get the matter settled soon.'

'What if we refuse?' Leonie asked huskily.

Argon shrugged. 'I shall leave everything to you.'

She swallowed. 'I could refuse the inheritance.'

'I will provide for that contingency. I can always leave my money to found museums, remember.'

She was horrified. 'You can't mean you would cut Paul out altogether! Leave the money away from the family?'

Argon's jaw set. 'I mean just that.'

'He could dispute the will,' she protested.

Argon laughed. 'Paul would not do that. He has too much pride.'

'I would not dispute it,' Paul agreed flatly. He turned at last and stared at Argon with a stony face. 'As to my pride, do you really think I would sell myself to my cousin for your money?'

'If you marry Leonie the money becomes yours,' Argon said softly.

Paul's face stiffened. Leonie was bewildered. 'But ...' she began.

Argon held up a veined hand. 'Paul will have to have your consent, however, to make any major changes in the companies, and he could make no large withdrawals without your consent, either.'

'In fact, although I would nominally own Caprels Leonie would have the final say in decisions,' Paul suggested icily.

Argon nodded. 'Exactly. I would leave real control in Leonie's hands, but you would be master of Comus.'

Paul laughed bitterly. 'An empty title, however.'

'The choice is yours,' said Argon. 'I am tired now. Come back later and tell me what you have decided to do.'

They left the room in silence. Paul led the way down to the garden and stood on the bright, smooth lawn staring at the sky with a guarded expression.

'He can't be serious,' Leonie said, growing tired of the moody silence.

'Argon never makes idle jokes about money.' Paul thrust his hands deep into his pockets. He paced to and fro with the restless gait of a tiger, then turned suddenly and faced her. 'Well? What shall we do?'

She stared at him wide-eyed. 'Do? Why, we refuse, of course. You couldn't allow him to dictate your life like that.'

'So you will get the Caprel money,' Paul said coolly. 'My dear cousin, congratulations.'

She went white. 'I shan't accept it, don't worry.'

'Greece will acquire a wonderful new museum, then.'

'I just don't believe he would do that,' she protested. 'He's too fond of you.'

'Where business is concerned Argon has no emotions. He has found me wanting. He will not change his mind now.'

'I wish I'd never come here,' she whispered.

'Too late to wish the past undone,' Paul said crisply. He glanced at her out of empty blue eyes. 'Again I ask you, cousin. What will you do? The decision must be yours.'

She met his eyes hesitantly. 'Are you suggesting that we accept this marriage?'

'I am suggesting that I am willing to marry you if you wish it.'

'You would do that for the money?'

His face set like marble. 'My reasons are my own business. You must make the choice.'

'I have a right to know the reason for your decision,' she insisted. 'Earlier you seemed adamant in refusing. Why have you changed your mind?'

'Perhaps I don't share your rooted objection to arranged marriages,' he said.

'You've changed your tune suddenly. Didn't you say you would never sell yourself for money?' The words flew out before she had considered them and she wished she could recall them, but too late. Paul's set cold face warned her that he resented being reminded of his words.

'I've had time to think, perhaps,' he said, dropping the words in glacial syllables.

'Oh, was that all it needed?' She felt a surge of wounded rage as she looked at his wild, handsome, sullen face. She had respected him when he refused to consider marrying her in order to regain his posi-

tion as heir to the Caprel fortune, but now she bitterly despised him once more. 'A little time goes by
and you're ready to put yourself up for auction? A
pretty plaything for a rich woman? Well, I suppose
the way you've lived so far has prepared you for
such a bargain. I expect you've bought love yourself
before now. But I am not accustomed to the ambi-
ence of the love market. I've never considered
purchasing a human being before.'

Paul's face slowly hardened into a golden mask
out of which his brilliant blue eyes glittered icily at
her. 'Then you will have to consider it now.'

Leonie turned away angrily and moved towards
the end of the garden and the start of the beach path.
She wanted to be alone to think, to work out what it
was she really felt. Paul followed her swiftly. Out of
sight of the house, under the shifting shade of the
pine trees, he caught up with her and stopped her in
her tracks, his hands gripping her shoulders.

'Let go of me! I can do without your company.
How can I think when you're with me?'

'Do I disturb you, my dear?' he asked softly.

'You annoy me,' she flung back. 'You're spoilt,
odious and spineless!'

'Thank you,' he said very quietly. 'Obviously I'm
a poor bargain for you.' The blue eyes stabbed her.
'A pretty plaything of little value, I gather. No
wonder you're not in a hurry to pay the purchase
price.' His mouth twisted wryly. 'Especially since
you can have the Caprel fortune without the annoy-
ance of marrying me.'

She winced. 'Oh, stop feeling sorry for yourself!'
She felt a black misery oppressing her, and she was
too tired to examine the reasons for this misery. She
only knew that she wished she had never come here,
never met Paul or Argon. Had she had any suspicions as to her great-grandfather's plan she would
have stayed in England. A loose lock of black hair
drifted from its moorings and fell over her pale face.
She pushed it back out of the way and it floated
down again a moment later. Paul deftly pushed it
back into its pin, his long fingers lingering on her
hair. She shivered.

For some reason this appeared to enrage him even
further. He shot back from her, stiffening. 'I'm sorry
you find my very touch repulsive,' he said angrily. 'If
the idea of the intimate side of marriage is a
stumbling block we can always make a pact to keep
our marriage purely platonic.'

This seemed to Leonie to be so insulting that she
barely knew how to answer him. Her throat was stiff
with outrage. In a low, bitter voice, she said, 'I
assure you that if I did agree to this absurd proposal,
it would only be on that condition.'

Paul laughed harshly. 'Naturally. A marriage of
convenience, then, on both sides.'

'Leaving us both free to have the marriage annulled if we want to marry someone else,' she added,
feeling the desperation of one who is burning her
home down rather than surrender it to an enemy.

'Agreed.' Paul pushed his hands into his pockets
and rocked on his heels. 'Is it a deal, then?'

She hesitated. 'You're rushing me,' she protested.

'Argon will want a reply as soon as possible,' he said.

She made a gesture of despairing resignation. 'Oh, very well.'

Paul spun on his heel and walked back towards the house without another word. Leonie, overwhelmed by a sudden feeling of sick anxiety, called out to him to wait. 'I'm not sure ... I can't ... I need more time.'

He did not turn or even appear to hear her, striding on at a speed that soon took him out of sight. Leonie sank down on the earth and weakly burst into tears.

The events of the last hour had been too much for her nerves. This visit to Comus had been a sufficient strain without the addition of such a burden. Argon's arbitrary decision had taken her breath away. She could not believe him to be serious at first, but once realising that he meant every word, she had barely time to think about his plan before he had gone further and completely stunned her with his suggestion that she marry Paul.

Her childhood adoration of her cousin had left her with a certain hidden softness towards him of which she was only partially aware. Argon's suggestion outraged this secret tenderness just as too early a spring can sometimes blight a flower. Had she been as indifferent to him as she had pretended she would not have been so disturbed, but faced with the necessity to choose or reject him as a husband she had been made miserable by an unadmitted feeling that she was ruining her chances of happiness with him. Paul was a proud man, and he would not enjoy being put in this position. Their relationship would never be the same again.

Some time later she returned to the house, having scrubbed from her face all traces of tears. She found Paul in Argon's room. Argon held out a gnarled, blue-veined hand to her, smiling warmly.

'Paul has told me. I am very pleased, my dear. You will see, all will work out very well in the end.'

She allowed him to kiss her cheek, trying not to meet Paul's eye. She was filled with embarrassment at the sight of him.

'The wedding shall be soon,' Argon said. 'I have little time. I want to see you safely married before I die.'

'You're not going to die,' she told him gently.

He sighed. 'My doctor has given me three months, my dear, no longer.'

She was stricken. 'Oh, Argon! Why didn't you tell us? You must have a second opinion. He may be wrong.'

Argon shook his head. 'He is as good a doctor as I am likely to find anywhere in the world. No, he only told me what I knew already. That is why I am in such a hurry. I want my estate settled before I go.' He took her hand and firmly handed it to Paul, who held it lightly between both of his. 'There! Kiss her, Paul, to seal the bargain.'

Stiff and white-faced, Leonie lifted her face. Paul's mouth brushed hers, cold as ice against her lips. Both of them knew that troubled waters lay ahead.

CHAPTER THREE

It was Argon's decision to make the wedding a quiet ceremony which would take place on Comus itself. He explained to Leonie that if they had the ceremony in Athens he would have to invite a great many people whom he had no longer any wish to meet. 'Although I have so few close relations, I have many distant ones, all of whom would expect to be invited to your wedding—not to mention my old friends and acquaintances, who are legion! I am too tired to go through all that. All I want is to see you married to Paul here in our own little church, according to the ancient rites.' He surveyed her anxiously. 'You will marry Paul in our church, my dear? I know your aunt has brought you up in the English church, but our family has always been Orthodox and the people on Comus would not understand if you did not agree to be married as all the Caprels have been.'

'I don't know much about your religion,' she said hesitantly.

Argon gestured warmly. 'I will ask our priest to speak to you and explain something of what it means. Father Basil is a good man. You will like him.'

Paul drove her down to the church on a warm afternoon when the shadows beneath the olive trees were black as night and the air hung motionless above the hillside. There was no breath of wind. Even the sea seemed hushed.

The little church of St Sophia was built of ancient grey stone in the familiar onion style of architecture. A windbattered gilt cross glittered on the dome.

'It's medieval,' Paul explained. 'The people have worshipped here for centuries, and our family have enriched it with many icons.'

The interior was gratefully cool—small, dark and yet lit magically by the glitter of the rows of silver icons facing the door. Candles burnt before the icons, row upon row of them. Paul explained that people lit them for many reasons; a mother praying for another child, a father praying that his wife might have a son, a bereaved family praying for peace for their dead relative. The little blue lights leapt up, reflected in the silver blaze behind them. The icons were of favourite saints. It was the custom, Paul told Leonie, to donate an icon to the church whenever a prayer had been granted beyond reasonable hope. Everyday prayers did not need such expensive gratitude, but people felt impelled to give another icon when a special prayer was answered favourably. As he talked to her he lit a whole row of candles, then prayed silently for a moment, his golden head bent reverently, before kissing an icon of St Sophia. She guessed his prayers to be for Argon and was touched. She felt a desire to light a candle herself. There was a touching beauty in the practice.

Father Basil joined them a moment later. Tall,

thin and black-bearded, he wore a long black cas-
sock and a black hat. Paul explained why they were
there, and Father Basil's face lit up with pleasure.

'I shall be most happy to perform the ceremony,
he told them. He kissed Paul on both cheeks. 'I am
very glad of this, Paul. Very glad.' Then he smiled at
Leonie. 'If he is not good to you, come to me and I
will put the fear of God into him!'

Paul asked him to give Leonie some instruction in
the Greek faith, and he agreed at once. 'When can
you come and see me? It is best if we have a short
discussion once a week until the wedding, say, half
an hour each time. I am free between eleven and
eleven-thirty on Tuesday mornings. Would that be
convenient?'

She agreed that it would, and after refusing his
offer of a glass of citrus, they left.

'I think we should talk,' Paul said as they drove
back to the house. 'Come for a swim—we'll get
more privacy on the beach. Up at the house, Clyte
hears everything and carries it to Argon.'

They collected swimming things and made their
way down to the beach. They swam together, splash-
ing and diving in a friendly way, although each
aware of an invisible barrier between them.

Later they lay on their towels and sunbathed.
Leonie was desperately aware of Paul lying next to
her, his naked brown chest panting a little after his
vigorous exertion in the water. His body was still
wet, the drops glistening on his tanned skin, his
blond hair darkened with the water. Her breath
came fiercely as he shifted on to his side to look at her.

'You're very quiet,' he commented.

'There isn't much to say,' she responded.

He laughed briefly. 'I'd forgotten that you never waste breath on small talk. I think it's time we found out more about each other.'

She shrugged. 'I already know a lot about you, you forget.'

He grimaced. 'Sorry. I'd forgotten.' His tone held a new irony. 'I'll have to remember in future that you've been keeping a file on me.'

The truth of that made her jump, her skin flushing hotly, and his blue eyes narrowed. 'You look almost guilty. Did I hit the nail on the head, by any chance?'

She tried to laugh. 'I was curious enough about my mother's family to cut out a few items about you from the newspapers when I was a child.'

'You astonish me,' he said drily. 'I hadn't thought you were that interested.'

'You were the only member of my mother's family I had a chance to learn about. Argon never made the papers much.'

His smile was wry. 'No, he was always very circumspect.' He eyed her thoughtfully. 'So you kept a scrapbook about me. Learn much?'

'Mainly the names of your lady friends,' she retorted.

He flickered a teasing glance at her. 'All enchanting creatures too, if I recollect correctly.'

'And I'm sure you do.'

'What about you? Apart from your recent tragedy, what sort of men have you had in your life?'

'I was at art school for three years,' she said.

His pale eyebrows lifted. 'Art students? A wild bunch, from my experience.'

'They enjoyed life,' she murmured.

'Hmm...' Paul flicked sand on to her naked stomach. 'There's a distinct note of pleasurable reminiscence in your voice. Do I gather that you shared their enjoyment?'

'I didn't lead the life of a nun.'

He stiffened, his blue gaze holding hers, a stunned look on his face. 'Are you telling me that...?'

She laughed. 'No, I haven't been promiscuous. That wasn't what I meant. There was no one special at art school, just a noisy friendly lively crowd of young people. I joined in the general activities.'

He began to brush the sand off her skin. The movements made her tingle, intensely aware of the touch of those long, brown fingers. 'So,' he murmured. 'You were at a boarding school for years, then you went to college. Quite a restricted life. No real home, I suppose.'

'My aunt did her best, but...' She shrugged.

'Poor Leonie,' he said softly. 'After we are married, where would you like to live?'

She was startled. 'But ... I thought ... here.

He laughed. 'On Comus? My dear girl, I'm a businessman. I have to live somewhere a damned sight more convenient than a remote Greek island. It suits Argon to stay here all the year round, but he's old now. He is making his soul. But we shall have to choose one of the capital cities. I'm ready to fall in with any views you have. Paris, London, New

York—you can decide.'

She was dazzled by the idea of choosing a home in any city in the world.

He laughed at her expression. 'You look as if someone had poleaxed you! May I make a suggestion? If you disagree, you only have to say so ...'

'Yes?'

'You'll probably want to have a home in England, so I suggest we start looking for a nice house in the country there, but for the moment settle down in my Paris flat. It would be convenient because it's already decorated and furnished, and if you didn't like it we could take our time in finding somewhere else.'

'Oh, I would love to live in Paris for a while,' she agreed.

'Then it's agreed?'

She nodded. 'Yes.'

He stretched out on his back again, his lids lowered. 'Good. That's settled, then.' He yawned. 'Mmm, it's so hot out here! I feel like a lizard.'

Very daring, Leonie put out a hand and touched his naked shoulder. 'You don't feel like one,' she murmured.

Paul's muscles stiffened under her touch, but he made no response, and, shrinking, she snatched her hand away. The friendly, relaxed atmosphere which had begun to build up between them seemed suddenly to have evaporated, and she furiously regretted having stepped over the line they had invisibly drawn between them. Paul had made the effort to be pleasantly co-operative, but now her own folly had conjured up the ghost of their forced marriage, bringing down an iron curtain. Paul's pride must have suffered a serious blow when he agreed to the marriage. It would be a long time before he got over it.

From contrition she passed to pain and anger. Aloud, she said, 'We could always live apart after the marriage. Argon isn't to know whether I'm with you in Paris or back in my London flat.'

Paul flung round on her, his face taut with rage. 'Never suggest such a thing again! It's bad enough to have agreed to a platonic marriage. I'm not cheating on Argon beyond that.'

He stood up. 'We'd better get back to the villa before we quarrel disastrously.'

She followed him, mutely raging, until it occurred to her that they must look to an observer like a typical Greek married couple: the husband stalking ahead, the wife shuffling along in his wake. She began to giggle quietly, and Paul swung round again to eye her and demand to know what was funny.

'Nothing,' she snorted.

'If you're laughing at me,' he threatened, 'I shall teach you a lesson, my girl!'

Half hysterical by now, she darted past him and sped the rest of the way at a tremendous speed with Paul running after her. They burst into the house, Paul just behind her, reaching for her, and came face to face with Clyte. A sly grin flitted over the old woman's dark face.

'Ah, you have fun?' she asked them with amusement.

Panting and puffing, Leonie nodded. 'Great fun,' she retorted.

Paul muttered something which sounded remarkably like a swear word, and vanished up the stairs.

'I wonder what he said,' Leonie said wistfully, staring after him.

'Don't ask!' Clyte urged her. 'It was a Greek word which I would not care to translate.'

Leonie giggled. 'Poor Paul!'

Clyte's eyes lit with a smile. 'Yes, poor Paul. He has much to learn.'

So, Leonie discovered, had she when she met Father Basil as arranged in the church. He taught her the history and rituals of his religion week by week, giving her many books to read and awakening in her a desire to learn more about the history of Greece itself.

The wedding ceremony itself was long and complicated, but Leonie was enchanted to have the various observances explained to her. The date of the wedding was now settled upon, and she had accepted Argon's offer of a loaned wedding dress. He had kept his own wife's dress wrapped in tissue paper in a large chest, and Clyte gently brought it out to show it to Leonie. The ivory colour had faded to a soft creamy shade, but the lace was deliciously frothy and the style had a traditional element which pleased Leonie very much. Paul was astonished by Argon's suggestion, and protested that Leonie had the right to a wedding dress of her own, but Leonie insisted that she loved the dress.

'Wedding dresses haven't changed much in fifty

years. The only difference is that this one has got real French lace on it, and is exquisitely cut and sewn. I've never seen such tiny stitches. I shall be very proud to wear it. I couldn't find anything better anywhere in the world.'

'My wife made it with her own hands,' Argon told her.

'I only hope I don't burst her beautiful hand-sewn seams,' Leonie smiled. 'She must have had an incredibly tiny waist.'

'A hand's span,' Argon agreed proudly. 'But she looked like Paul, you know, a blonde and beautiful Greek with blue eyes.'

'So that's how he got his colouring!'

Argon smiled. 'That is how!'

On her wedding morning Leonie woke early with a sinking sensation in her stomach, too tense to eat the coffee and rolls Clyte brought up to her room.

Clyte helped her to dress, her old fingers shaking slightly. Leonie looked at herself in the mirror with dazed, incredulous eyes. The ivory silk had been washed and dried in the sun and was almost restored to its original colour. The bodice was demurely buttoned up to the tight little collar of lace and ribbon. The waistline was so tight-fitting that she could hardly breathe, but the full swell of the skirts gave her a much better outline. Lace and ribbon were showered upon the skirt and flounced it at the hem. Clyte lent her a blue ruched garter as a last thought, before flicking down the filmy lace veil over her face.

'I'm frightened,' Leonie whispered, clinging to the old woman's hand.

'Be brave, my darling,' Clyte whispered back, squeezing her fingers. 'You look like a goddess.'

The idea made Leonie smile and lightened her sudden qualm. She followed Clyte downstairs with legs which trembled slightly.

Argon was waiting for her in the long saloon. Paul, he informed her, had already left for the church. Argon took her hand and said softly, 'You are beautiful, my dear. I envy Paul.' Then he opened a flat leather box and took out a triple string of pearls and diamonds, clasping it round her throat with hands which shook a little.

'Oh! How lovely!' She touched the stones with trembling fingers. 'But I can't...'

'They are yours, my dear. They were my wife's, and I have kept them for Paul's wife. Wear them today.'

She kissed him. 'Thank you. They're lovely.' She went over to an ornate french mirror hanging on the wall and looked at herself, seeing a fine-boned dark girl with passionate eyes and mouth, her slender body sheathed in the ivory silk, her throat ablaze with diamonds and milky little pearls. 'I don't recognise myself. I feel so strange.'

They drove to the church, not in the silver limousine, but in a traditional open carriage, brought out of retirement for the occasion, its leather work dusted, its wheels picked out in gay yellow. Ribbons fluttered from the horses' brasses and white feathers nodded on their sleek heads. Leonie was delighted. She felt as though she had moved back in time to an earlier century.

The church was crowded to the doors with people. The scent of incense filled the air and row upon row of candles burnt along the wall before the silver icons.

The barbaric, dark faces of the saints watched over the wedding ceremony. The people intoned the responses deeply, so that Leonie felt they were all taking part in a serious way. Stealing a glance at Paul, kneeling beside her on a velvet hassock, she found him equally serious. His blond head was brushed to a smooth sheen, and he wore morning dress, which looked oddly formal on him. She was dazzled by his amazing good looks.

Commanded by the priest, they turned to kiss each other, their mouths lightly brushing.

Then they were returning down the aisle hand in hand, Leonie's veil thrown back and a crown of flowers resting lightly on her head, to the joyful triumph of the organ and the high sweet singing of the choir. The scent of the incense still floated around her from the moment when the priest had wafted it over them, and the blessings the priest had conferred seemed to hover over their heads. Although she had only learnt a little Greek so far, she had been able to follow the ceremony after her weeks of preparation, and she was glad that she had agreed to go through with it when she saw the bright, smiling faces of the people outside the church. They were so happy in her happiness that tears pricked at her eyes.

Children flung rose petals and rice, there were teasing shouts from the men and laughter from the women, then she and Paul were alone in the beribboned carriage, driving back to Comus Villa.

She had almost forgotten that this marriage was to be no real marriage. The rites and traditions had taken over, compelling emotions she had not expected.

Paul leaned back with a sigh. 'My God! That was an exhausting experience.'

She laughed, flushed and excited. 'Oh, but it was beautiful, too.'

'You were beautiful,' he said lightly. 'You looked superb in that dress. It could have been made for you.'

'Thank you,' she said, blushing even more pink.

He stared, his eyes focussing on her necklace. 'I see Argon gave you the necklace. He told me he would. Diamonds suit you.' He put up a finger to touch the stones and she began to tremble. A hot awareness of him grew inside her. She lowered her eyes and stared at the lace on her skirts.

They arrived back at the villa. Taking up a stand by the door, they received the islanders, shaking hands with one after another, smiling endlessly, receiving congratulations and laughing at the little jokes the men made slyly. Leonie hardly understood most of what was said, but she took her cue from Paul and smiled when he smiled.

The wedding breakfast was copious and elaborate. Leonie still could not touch a bite of food. Her tension seemed to increase rather than diminish as the day wore on. They cut the huge cake to shouts of pleasure, giving the first slice to Argon, then Paul and Leonie opened the dancing together, while the party clapped and smiled.

Leonie's head was whirling as Paul danced her around the long room, her skirts flying out against his thighs. Hunger and excitement made her almost faint.

Her golden eyes were huge in her white face, she clung to his broad shoulder desperately, trying to keep up with him, hoping she would not be swallowed up in the faint mist she seemed to see swimming before her eyes.

The others began to join in the dancing, their feet stamping on the marble floor. Paul looked down at her, his expression full of concern. 'You're very pale. Are you feeling all right?'

'I'm feeling dizzy,' she smiled, her dark head swaying slightly like a flower on a long white stem.

'Sit down,' he urged, propelling her towards a chair. Leonie fell into it giddily, her eyes closing. The room seemed to revolve faster and faster. She clung to Paul's hands in an effort to stabilise herself. Her ears were filled with a soft roaring sound, like the noise one hears in a seashell placed against the ear. Her limbs were cold and heavy. She fought to retain consciousness.

A glass suddenly touched her lips and the odour of brandy drifted to her nostrils.

'Drink this,' Paul murmured.

Leonie obediently sipped, making a little grimace at the taste. A burning sensation stung in her throat and chest, but her head began to clear.

'She has hardly eaten a morsel all day.' Clyte's voice, soft and anxious. 'I saw she was on the verge of fainting.'

'Thank you for the brandy,' Paul replied warmly. 'I didn't like to leave her.'

'She must eat,' Clyte said. 'I'll fetch some food.'

Paul's thumb rubbed gently over the back of Leonie's hand. 'Little fool,' he murmured. 'Why didn't you eat? How do you feel now?'

She slowly opened her lids and found herself seated at the end of the saloon, beside the open door, protected from curious eyes by Paul's back. He knelt in front of her, looking at her watchfully.

She offered him a slight smile. Although her giddiness had retreated it had left her weak, and a languid feeling pervaded her whole body.

'I'll be fine,' she murmured faintly.

'You are as white as a ghost, as white as your dress,' he told her with muted anger. 'Don't ever do anything so silly again!'

Clyte hobbled back with a plate of sandwiches. Paul took them from her and selected one, lifting it to Leonie's lips.

'I can't...' she whispered, turning her head away.

'You can and you will,' Paul insisted firmly.

Moistening her lips with the tip of her tongue, she permitted him to insert the sandwich, then nibbled a corner of it reluctantly. It tasted like sawdust, but Paul's grim expression forced her to go on eating until she had consumed the whole sandwich. The food had a slow effect. Gradually she began to feel stronger, and her hunger became acute. While Clyte and Paul watched approvingly, she finished the whole plateful of sandwiches.

'That's better,' Paul nodded.

He stood up, his hand pulling her up too, and moved towards the open door, supporting her by an arm around her waist. Clyte followed.

Paul led her upstairs to her room. Clyte vanished into the room while Paul looked down at Leonie, his face impassive. 'Change your dress now. We're leaving.'

She was staggered. 'Leaving? But ... where? Paris already?'

His mouth twisted ironically. 'No, my darling wife. On our honeymoon.'

Scarlet flooded her face. 'Honeymoon?' she whispered hoarsely. 'What on earth do you mean?'

'It is customary to have a honeymoon after a wedding,' he pointed out.

'But we ... our marriage isn't ...' Her throat closed rawly on the words.

'Our marriage is in name only?' He finished for her, his eyes sardonic. 'Of course. But we have to keep up appearances, don't we? So we must have a honeymoon. I've made all the arrangements. We'll spend a week in a little house in the hills, a remote and lonely little house.' His eyes mocked her. 'I apologise for the necessity, but in the circumstances I thought somewhere remote would be best. It will spare us the problem of trying to appear deliriously happy. There'll be no one for us to impress. There'll be plenty of simple food. We can look after ourselves, make our beds, wash up, and so on...'

Her nerves leapt wildly at the prospect. She had difficulty in answering him. Faintly, she said, 'Very well, Paul.'

'Wear something pretty,' he said quickly, as she turned away to enter her room.

She looked at him in surprise, and he grinned at her. 'The people downstairs will want to give us a send-off in traditional style. They'll feel cheated if the bride doesn't look absolutely ravishing.'

Clyte was standing beside the wardrobe, scanning Leonie's clothes doubtfully. Leonie joined her and surveyed them with an equally depressed eye. It had not occurred to her to buy anything special for this occasion. A trip to Athens to buy clothes had been suggested by Argon, but she had gently refused the offer. Now she wished she had accepted.

In the end she chose a rose-pink dress with a tight waist, full skirt and balloon-like chiffon sleeves. It was the only dress she had which was suitable for a special occasion. Clyte nodded approval, but pressed the gay floral crown back on to Leonie's black hair.

'They will expect you to wear a hat!'

'I look ridiculous,' Leonie protested, giggling.

Clyte shook her head, smiling. 'Very pretty,' she insisted.

Paul was standing outside the door, having changed quickly into a formal dark suit. He studied Leonie in enigmatic silence, then nodded. 'Yes, you'll do!'

'Well, thank you,' she returned sarcastically.

His blue eyes flashed amusement. 'The only thing wrong is the expression,' he said lightly. 'You look too rebellious for a happy bride. Try to look demurely ecstatic.'

'Sure you don't want me to crawl after you on my knees too?' she demanded furiously.

'No,' he said with an air of reluctant dismissal. 'No, I don't think you need to go that far. But remember, I have a position to keep up. These people have a very old-fashioned attitude to the relationship between man and wife. In Greece it's the man who governs the household. I wouldn't want to lose face in their eyes by appearing to have no control over my wife.'

'Oh,' she raged, her fists clenched at her side. 'Oh, I would dearly like to hit you!'

He laughed. 'Later, my darling. Later.'

Their arrival downstairs was the signal for an outburst of noisy welcome. They were clapped and cheered, showered with flowers and whispered blessings from the women, with advice and winks from the men. Argon came towards them slowly, leaning on the arms of two tall, strong men. He kissed them both, tears in his eyes. Leonie flung her arms around his neck and kissed him on the cheek, her eyes wet too.

Then they were outside, escaping from a laughing little crowd of wellwishers. The carriage was waiting there, still beribboned and decked. Paul helped her into the seat, picked her floral crown from her head and flung it into the little group of young girls. Their hands grabbed for it and they shrieked eagerly. One caught it and held it aloft in triumph, and everyone clapped.

Then they were moving, the horses trotting briskly, and soon the noise of the wedding party had died away behind them. Leonie collapsed against the seat. Paul took her hand and squeezed it, and she glanced at him in wary surprise. He winked towards their driver, a black-haired, slim young man.

She gathered that he wished her to continue to keep up appearances.

Tenderly he enquired, 'Tired, my darling?'

'Yes,' she agreed tightly, longing to kick his ankle. The loving note in his voice infuriated her, especially when she could see a glint of mockery in the blue eyes.

Paul lifted her hand to his lips, softly turning his mouth against her palm. Leonie quivered, half in anger, half in reluctant response.

The carriage turned on to a rough, stony track which led up between two stark hills. Goats with belled necks bounded from slope to slope, bleating softly. A hawk circled above them, making a shrill discordant sound of protest at their invasion of his territory. Soon the path grew too steep and difficult for the horses. Their hooves slipped on the stones and the carriage dragged slowly foot by foot.

Paul spoke to the driver, who halted, clucking at his two horses.

'We must walk the rest of the way,' Paul told her. 'Alex will bring the rest of the luggage up.' He helped her down, climbed down himself and took two bags from the luggage rack on the back of the carriage.

The driver brought the rest. Clyte had packed the bags for Leonie during the wedding party, it seemed. Leonie wondered what clothes she had packed. None of her dresses had been missing, so presumably Clyte had packed jeans and skirts.

The little house stood sheltered from the wind in a hollow of the hills, facing the sea hundreds of feet below, with a small grove of olives hidden behind it out of the wind. The thick stone walls were white-washed, the roof roughly thatched with dried turf. A hen-house and a small enclosure full of goats indi-cated that Paul had borrowed the house from one of the farmers. Leonie wondered if they were expected to look after the animals. Had Paul not said that they would be alone? She had never milked a goat and she hoped she was not going to be asked to start now.

Alex left the luggage in the one little room down-stairs, gave them both a broad smile and wished them well in Greek. Paul thanked him gravely, and Leonie smiled at him.

Then he had gone and they were alone. A silence fell. Leonie could hear the wind whistling through the olives and the distant whisper of the sea. Ner-vously, she looked around the low, dark room. There were only two windows, both rather small, and the rapidly dying light left them in semi-twilight.

'We'll need a fire,' Paul said. 'It gets cold up here in the early hours of the morning.'

While he sought out kindling she explored the

downstairs area. There were two cheap easy chairs,
a table and chairs, a cabinet filled with china and
cooking utensils and a large, ominously old cooking
range.

Paul returned and soon had a fire alight. She
noticed that he used a mixture of turf and sticks.
The fire smoked a little, but soon began to warm the
cold room.

'The larder is outside,' Paul told her, indicating a
back door.

Leonie investigated and discovered a large stone
room filled with jars and earthenware crocks, tins
and various fresh foods.

'We'll have a cold meal tonight,' Paul suggested.
'Some of that cheese, bread and cold lamb.'

Obediently she carried food into the sitting-room,
laid the table and they sat down to eat. The goats'
cheese was unfamiliar, but palatable, and they followed it with pitta, heated over the fire until it was
hot and smoke-blackened. The cold lamb had a
smoky flavour too, and Paul told her it had been
roasted whole over a fire outside, by the look of it. It
was a favourite way of cooking lamb in these parts.

They ended with fruit: grapes, and imported
oranges which Paul had had sent up here earlier for
them.

Paul made coffee in a battered old tin coffee pot
on the range. With the range fire going, the room
was growing overheated, so he piled more turf on to
the fire so that its heat gradually died down to a
slow glow.

Yawning, Leonie glanced at the narrow, dark

little stairs. The candles Paul had lit gave only a slight illumination. Judging by the size of the downstairs room, she was anxiously wondering if there was also only one room upstairs.

'Tired?' Paul asked, helping her clear the table. 'Why not go up to bed? I'll wash up and tidy down here.'

'I'll help,' she protested, but he insisted, so, taking a candle, she made her way up the stairs.

The long, low room upstairs was dominated by one large bed covered by a woven bedspread. Leonie stood very still, staring around her, her pulses leaping.

Where did Paul intend to sleep?

She undressed and climbed into bed some time later, shivering with nerves rather than the cold.

When she heard Paul's foot on the stair she sat up and stared at the black shadow he made on the wall as he approached, a huge, terrifying profile etched against the candlelight.

Paul looked at her across the room, his hands thrust into his pockets.

'Where are you going to sleep?' she asked shakily.

Silently he glanced at the pillow beside her.

Trembling, she flung angry words at him. 'Marriage of convenience, you said? Remember? Purely platonic. I might have known this set-up was coming, that you would try something underhand and sneaky. I should have known better than to trust you!' She drew a hard, troubled breath. 'Well, whatever your plan for tonight you can forget it! I'm not sharing this bed with you. So get out of here, and don't think that because we're alone up here at the back of the world you can take advantage of your superior strength, because I warn you, if you lay one finger on me I'll put up enough of a fight to make you regret your hollow victory!'

He had listened without moving to this speech, his honey-gold head tilted, his face masked in shadows. When she was silent, he strolled slowly forward and gave her a cool, barbed smile.

'My dear, what makes you think I am even tempted to break my word? If you will give me some of your bedclothes and that extra pillow, I'll make myself a bed downstairs.' His blue eyes insolently mocked her. 'As I had intended in the first place.'

She was stricken with remorse, realising that beneath his cool exterior he was furious at what she had said. 'Paul, I'm sorry...' Her stammered words were ignored as he bent forward to take the pillow and the woven bedspread from her. Forgetting that she wore only a brief cotton nightdress, cut low, with thin ribbon straps to hold it up, she climbed out of the bed and followed him across the room, apologising.

'I made a fool of myself—I realise that. It was a stupid, ridiculous mistake...' She caught at his sleeve to halt his relentless progress. 'Wait, Paul! Do listen!'

'God in heaven!' he shouted suddenly, flinging down the armful of bedclothes and swinging round towards her with eyes of glittering blue stone and a face savage with rage. 'Listen? What else have I been doing for the last ten minutes? I've run out of patience, Leonie. You've driven me beyond the point of reasonable endurance. First you insult me by implying that I have no sense of honour and would break my oath lightly, then you pursue me babbling like a fool about having made a little mistake!' The blue eyes flashed comprehensively over her long, slender body, only partially clothed in thin white cotton. 'Well, it seems to me that I might as well behave in the manner expected of me. I wouldn't like to disappoint a lady.'

'Paul...' she cried in protest as he swooped on her. 'Paul, please...'

He lifted her in his arms, his face stormy with temper, and carried her back across the room to the bed, flinging her down on it with a violent gesture. Before she had time to recover, he had blown out the candle and his body hurtled across the bed, crushing the breath out of her, his arms pinning her to the pillow as his mouth sought hers.

Raging, yet helpless beneath the heavy weight of his body, she struggled in vain to free herself, but Paul was remorseless. Slowly Leonie felt her own secret hunger leap up to meet his as his lips parted her mouth, demanding a response. For a few moments she fought her own desire as well as his, then, with a smothered groan of defeat, she surrendered, locking her arms behind his head.

Paul slid his mouth down her throat, one hand expertly pulling down the thin straps of her nightdress. She began to tremble as his lips burnt along her shoulder, down over her breasts, while his fingers explored freely, stroking and caressing her.

'Paul ... darling ...' her own voice sounded strange in her ears, hoarse with passion she had never felt before. Her heart was pounding as though it would burst. Her breath hurt in her lungs. A dizzy excitement taught her the responses of which until this moment she had been ignorant; her hands running down Paul's back, feeling him arch in pleasure, breathing fiercely against her naked flesh.

Her senses clamoured for release from the spiralling hunger he had aroused, but suddenly Paul sat up, still breathing hard, and said savagely, 'I hope that has taught you a lesson.'

She lay as he had left her, her black hair loose around her face, her nightdress half off, her body still quivering from the last few moments. Shock kept her silent.

'I could take you now, and you would be more than willing,' Paul told her icily. 'Next time you're tempted to lecture me on morals, my darling, remember that! I can get you to abandon all your principles in the space of ... what? Five minutes?'

Anger began to churn in the pit of her stomach— anger and bitter shame. She said nothing, lying there in the darkness, stiff with self-disgust and outrage.

Paul moved away, picked up the bedclothes from the floor where he had flung them, and vanished.

Leonie stared into the blackness of the room and hated him with a hatred which was part despair, part self-loathing. She knew that she would never forget, never forgive him for what had just happened, for what he had just said.

CHAPTER FOUR

THIN needles of light penetrated the room at dawn, pricking Leonie awake. She had fallen asleep with difficulty, and her eyes were still pink-rimmed from weeping. She lay watching the room gradually swim out of the darkness, too weary to get up.

A muffled clatter from below made her suddenly aware that Paul was moving about. She slid out of bed, put on a cotton wrap-over gown and went downstairs. As she had discovered last night, there was no bathroom. Paul had shown her the clear, pebble-bottomed stream which ran down behind the olive grove and provided the only source of fresh water. She did not much relish the prospect of washing there this morning, but she had no choice.

Paul, in a blue shirt and faded old jeans, stood beside the blackened old range watching the coffee pot. He turned as he heard her footsteps, and their eyes met briefly.

'I'm sorry about last night,' he said abruptly. 'I lost my temper—I've no excuse. It was unforgivable.' There was a visible tension in his handsome tanned face. His mouth was taut, his eyes shadowed. Leonie guessed that he, like herself, had lost sleep.

'It doesn't matter,' she said, knowing she lied. The memory of those few moments was burned on her brain and she knew she would never forget them.

But they were up here alone in this isolated house for a week. It was necessary to re-establish some sort of truce. They could not exist in a state of enmity. It would make ordinary living impossible.

He watched her without illusions, reading her hidden reactions in her face. Heavily, he gestured to the coffee pot. 'Have some?'

'I want to wash first,' she said.

He nodded. 'Continental breakfast, I'm afraid. Hot pitta and coffee. Okay?'

'Fine,' she said lightly, moving out of the back door. The sun still lay just on the horizon, faintly illumining the hills with a blue-gold light. A purple haze crowned the highest peaks. The scent of pine trees, mixed with the fragrant odour of heather and dew-wet grass, made the air sweet to breathe. Leonie found her way to the stream through the olive grove, knelt down on the stony bank and splashed vigorously, stinging her face awake with the ice-cold water.

Ten minutes later, her black hair combed up into a neat coil, her slim body sheathed in a black shirt and jeans, she was eating breakfast.

'I thought we could take some food and go for a long walk across the hills,' Paul suggested. 'I'm afraid there isn't much to do up here.'

'I would like that,' she said quietly.

They washed up, tidied the house, found some meat, cheese and bread and set off just as the sun came swimming up above the sea.

She was glad to have her body and mind occupied by the exercise. She had no time to think. She was too busy clambering after Paul, who strode up the hillsides as though he were a goat, his long legs covering the ground at a staggering speed. Their path was littered with grey rocks fallen from above, and on the slopes beside it she could see the sturdy green sprigs of thyme which gave the hills their special fragrance. There was no habitation for miles around. All she could see was the sky, the sea and the great sweep of the hills, as ancient as the earth itself, their stark outlines untouched by man.

At noon they paused in the shade of a wild olive to eat their frugal meal. Paul had brought a bottle of retsina in the rucksack of food he had carried on his back. While Leonie lay back, panting, her head cushioned on a little bed of green moss kept fresh by a constant trickle of water from the rocky hillside stream above them, Paul laid out the food and opened the retsina. She accepted a mug of it from him, cautiously sipping the resin-impregnated wine and finding it curiously refreshing after her exertions.

Paul handed her a flat oval of pitta and a scoop of curdy goats' cheese pushed down inside the split bread. She gave him a polite little smile. 'Thank you.'

He almost winced, his blue eyes stormy. 'For God's sake, Leonie! Stop looking at me as if I were the wolf and you were Little Red Riding Hood. I've said I'm sorry about last night. I know an apology is hardly sufficient, but what else can I say or do? We can't go on like this. I'm not a patient man. I couldn't stand this state of warfare for long.'

'You can hardly blame me for feeling uneasy,' she pointed out, her voice husky.

'You provoked me into that outburst last night! I would never have behaved like that otherwise.'

She had to accept the truth of this accusation. Had she never lost her head because she jumped to conclusions he would not have lost his head in his turn. She sighed. 'I know I behaved very foolishly, but I was feeling nervous. The house is so isolated, and I was strung up after the wedding...'

'I realise that now,' he said gently.

'I'm sorry it happened,' she said.

'We both made fools of ourselves,' Paul murmured. 'Your mistake was more forgivable than mine, I realise.' He shot her a sidelong glance. 'Did I frighten you very much?'

Her lids lowered to hide the expression of her eyes. 'You were rather overpowering.'

He gave a harsh crack of laughter. 'Delightful English understatement! I take note of the implied irony.'

A smile twitched reluctantly at her lips.

Paul put out a slim brown hand. 'Pax?'

She slowly laid her fingers on top of his. 'Yes. Pax.'

'And we're friends again?'

'Were we friends?' she asked drily.

'Oh, Leonie,' he murmured reproachfully. 'Let us at least be friends! Surely we can be friends?'

His blue glance made her laugh. 'You think you're irresistible, don't you, Paul?'

He grinned lazily. 'Is that your considered opinion?'

'My considered opinion is that you're very spoilt,' she told him. 'Too much money, too many women ...'

His blue eyes teased. 'You resent the women?'

She flushed. 'Your life is your own affair.' And she remembered angrily how she had surrendered last night and how he had said that he was only teaching her a lesson, showing her that she was no different from all the other women in his life, that he could take her if he wished and she would be a willing victim. Beneath her calm exterior burned a desire for revenge on him for the shame he had inflicted on her. Never again, she vowed to herself, would he win that particular battle. She would die rather than lose her head again over him.

They sat eating their food in the shade for a while, then Paul rose, stretching his long limbs. 'Time we moved on, I'm afraid. Up here the sun becomes unbearable once noon is past. We must get back down to the house.'

The climb down was just as exhausting. Several times her feet slid from under her, and Paul's strong right arm came into service to catch and hold her. Each time she felt her heart stop at his touch, and each time she hated herself for her weakness.

They reached the house under the full glare of the afternoon sun. Heat bounced back from the rocks, dazzling her eyes. The sun hung overhead like a great brass coin. Pain throbbed at the back of her neck and she longed for the darkness and shade of the house.

'In Greece we find it most sensible to have a siesta in the afternoon,' he told her. 'Why don't you go upstairs and take a nap?'

'What a delightful idea,' she groaned, rubbing the back of her neck with one hand.

'Headache?' he said.

'Mmm...' she nodded, wincing with pain.

He came behind her and drew her head back with his hands. She stiffened, but relaxed as he began gently massaging the back of her neck, his long slender fingers deftly manipulating her muscles, unlocking them from their painful rigidity. She felt the iron grip of the pain unfold link by link, the throbbing in her head decrease and the red glare behind her eyes die slowly away. A deep sigh wrenched at her. 'Oh, that's lovely...'

'I'm glad you like it,' he whispered against her hair, his fingers still moving, but now with an intimate caressing movement which sent a wave of warm weakness down her spine.

She hurriedly stepped away from him. 'Thank you.' Her tone was stiff. 'My headache has gone now. I'll go up and take that nap.'

He watched her slender body move towards the stairs. Leonie glanced back once and caught a strangely serious look on his handsome face.

The shutters were up over the little windows in the bedroom. The room was dark and slightly stuffy, but much cooler than the sun-ravaged hillside.

She lay down on the bed and closed her eyes. A few moments later Paul materialised beside her with a cup of tea. He grinned as he put it down beside her. 'I thought this would make you feel more at home!'

She was touched. 'Oh, thank you! That's wonderful! Just what I need!'

He nodded and went out. Leonie sipped the tea gratefully, letting the refreshing flavour circulate around her mouth which was dry and filled with the dust of the hillside.

Moments later she was asleep, curled on her side like a child, one hand beneath her flushed cheek.

She woke with a start, feeling something touch her skin. Her eyes flew open. Paul stood beside her, an amused look on his face.

'You've slept like the dead. I've made our evening meal. Have a wash and come down to eat.' He indicated a tin bowl of steaming water standing on the little table beside her. 'I thought you might like some warm water, so I boiled the kettle for you.'

'You're very thoughtful,' she said. 'Thank you.' Glancing at her watch, she was astounded by the time. 'Goodness! I have slept well!'

'I shouldn't have taken you for such a long walk,' he said. 'You were exhausted, poor child.'

He went back downstairs. Leonie slid off the bed, stripped off her clothes and washed slowly and enjoyably, her skin delighting in the warm caress of the water.

Standing in her bra and panties, she hunted out a dress to wear, then a sound made her turn. Paul

stood behind her, his eyes fixed on her. She flushed
and instinctively pulled a dress down to cover herself
with, bringing a faint smile to his mouth.

'I've seen you in a bikini, remember,' he said
sardonically. 'You are no less unclothed now.'

'Would you please get out while I dress?'

'I came to ask you to hurry. The meat will spoil if
we don't eat soon.'

'I won't be a moment.'

He nodded, turned, then halted and said over his
shoulder, 'You have an enchanting body, Leonie.'

She flushed wordlessly. Then he was gone. Hastily
she put on the dress, the only one Clyte had packed,
a simple linen sleeveless dress she had made herself.
The style suited her and she loved the gay lemon
yellow colour, but she had had it for months and she
wished she had something more exciting to wear
tonight.

Paul had cooked kebabs over the charcoal range;
skewers of rosemary-flavoured lamb served on a bed
of salad with boiled rice. Leonie congratulated him
on his cooking and he grinned. 'Glad you like it.'

There was the usual retsina with the meal. She
was beginning to like the wine now. The unusual
flavour was growing on her. After her third glass
Paul hesitated, the bottle poised. 'Sure you want
another? It's deceptively mild, you know.'

'I'm totally unaffected by it,' she said cheerfully,
holding up her glass. She wanted to chase away the
faint depression which was threatening her, and
Paul's suggestion that she might find the wine too
strong irritated her.

He shrugged and poured her another glass. Then he got up and produced a cassette player powered by batteries. A moment later dreamy music filtered through the room and Leonie sighed with pleasure. 'That's nice.'

Paul pulled her up out of the chair. 'Dance with me,' he murmured, his arms sliding round her.

They moved slowly round the dark little room. The glow of the candles and the faint red of the fire showed them where they were going, but Leonie found the heat and stuffiness of the room making her drowsy once more. She sleepily let her head fall against Paul's broad shoulder, her arms locked round his neck. His thighs moved against her, his hands pressing her closer.

'This is nice,' she murmured drowsily.

'Isn't it?' said Paul, his mouth against her hair, one hand slowly stroking her back.

'You dance very well,' she said.

He laughed softly. 'Do I? Your hair smells of sunshine and grass.'

'That's nice,' she mumbled, her face pressed against his chest, feeling the heat of his body through the thin material of his shirt.

'Leonie, you're not falling asleep, are you?' he asked close to her ear, bending forward.

'No, certainly not,' she said indignantly, her knees slowly bending beneath her.

Paul laughed as she slid downwards, and scooped her up into his arms, lifting her like a doll, her black head thrown back. 'My God, you're drunk! That wine was too much for you.'

'Nonsense,' she said faintly. The room was dizzily spinning around her as Paul carried her up the stairs and into the bedroom. He paused, holding her, looking down at her flushed and sleepy face.

'Two glasses of retsina are your limit, I suspect,' he said with amusement.

'I am not drunk,' she said with great dignity.

His face was very close, the blue eyes brilliant beneath their fair brows. 'No?'

His mouth brushed hers lightly, the teasing flick of a butterfly kiss. Invaded by a warm pleasure, Leonie closed her eyes and waited for the touch of his mouth again, but he bent and laid her on the bed instead.

She locked her arms around his neck. 'Paul,' she whispered invitingly. 'Kiss me goodnight...'

He hesitated, then slowly lowered his mouth. Their mouths clung, passion flaring between them. Paul lay down beside her and began to kiss her more intently, his mouth parting her lips and sending shivers of weak delight down her spine.

'Darling,' he whispered against her neck. 'Oh, darling...' His hands wandered caressingly over her limp, relaxed limbs from breast to thigh while he kissed her mouth again then began to kiss her throat and shoulders. Leonie's eyes closed. She sighed once or twice, pleasurably.

Paul raised himself to look down at her, groaning. 'You shouldn't have drunk all that retsina. Have you forgotten we took a vow of non-consummation? Darling, I'm not made of stone. You're so sweet and desirable, and I...' He broke off abruptly at a

sound from her. 'What the—? Leonie?' He
peered closer, turning her head towards his eyes,
then swore softly under his breath. 'Asleep! My
God! I shall go out of my mind if this goes on...'

He lifted her heavy body with one arm while he
stripped off her dress, then slid her under the sheet.
She turned over in the bed so that her face burrowed
into the pillow, her arms going up to clasp it con-
fidingly. Paul touched the sleek black hair gently,
then moved towards the stairs, a frustrated grimace
on his face. Downstairs he stared at the unfinished
retsina, then, with a groan, picked it up and drained it
into a glass and swallowed it. Moments later silence
fell over the whole house as they both slept.

Leonie woke next morning with a feeling of happy
contentment. She had slept deeply all night, and she
had a distinct impression that her dreams had been
delightful ones, although she could not actually
remember any of them.

She stretched, yawning, then stiffened as she realised she was only wearing her bra and pants.

Frowning, she sat up and looked round the room.
Her dress was hung neatly over a chair. Yet she
could not remember undressing last night. She
thought back carefully. The last thing she could
positively recall was dancing with Paul in the dark.

What had happened after that? She shuddered to
imagine. Surely Paul would not have taken advantage of the fact that she had drunk too much?

She dressed in jeans and a shirt, and went downstairs. Paul was still asleep, rolled in the woven bedspread beside the fire, his honey-smooth blond hair

just visible. Leonie went out to the stream with the coffee pot and a towel. After washing briskly, she hurried back and put the coffee on while she sliced some bread. While she was asleep yesterday, Paul had fed the hens and retrieved their eggs, so she decided to boil some of the eggs for breakfast. They were tiny brown speckled eggs and looked inviting when they were ready in their yellow eggcups. The coffee ready, the table laid, she went over to arouse Paul.

He did not move when she said his name, so she bent over him to rouse him and found herself being pulled down on top of him.

'Paul!' she spluttered crossly. 'Let me go!'

His lips sought hers, and weakly, hating herself, she yielded. Warm, friendly, undemanding, the kiss was certainly pleasant, but she was alarmed to consider the implications lying behind it. What exactly had happened last night? Obviously, something had taken place, or why should he believe his kiss would be accepted?

She pushed him away, sat up, irritably tidying her hair, which had become unravelled during their little tussle. 'Breakfast is ready. Why don't you go and wash?'

He grinned. 'I'll do that, honey. Don't start without me.'

She sat at the table, sipping her steaming coffee. Paul was back a few moments later, fully dressed, his face glowing from the cool stream water. He dropped a light kiss on her head as he passed.

'Good morning again, darling.'

'Don't call me that!' she snapped.

He slid a sidelong look at her, brows raised ironically. 'Sorry, I didn't know you objected.'

'I dislike the use of endearments except when they're sincerely meant.'

'What makes you think I'm not sincere?'

She regarded him drily. 'Need you ask?'

'Oh, my reputation! You're like the elephant, aren't you? You never forget.' Then a smile danced along his handsome mouth. 'Except under very special circumstances.'

Hot colour burned in her cheeks. 'What happened last night?' she demanded huskily.

The blue eyes were amused. 'You don't remember?'

'Would I ask if I did?'

'Well now, that rather depends on whether you wanted to remember, doesn't it?'

'Why shouldn't I want to remember?' she asked, appalled.

He shrugged, one blue eye watching her secretly. 'How do I know?' He began to eat his breakfast, slicing off the top of his egg with one dexterous blow in a way which made her shiver. He was altogether too pleased with himself this morning. She had to know what really happened.

Slowly, she said, 'Well, I only remember dancing with you.'

He lifted her hand to his lips with a practised little bow. 'What came after that was much more enjoyable. What a pity you don't remember it!'

Grimly, she asked, 'Paul, for the last time, what did happen?'

He tasted his coffee and gave a sigh of pleasure. 'Mm ... quite delicious. You make good coffee. I'm glad about that. I'm a coffee addict and I ...'

'Paul!' Her nerves at snapping point, she broke in angrily.

He looked at her innocently. 'What's the matter?'

'Last night,' she repeated.

'You were enchanting,' he said.

She took a deep breath, her passionate face stormy. Her fingers curled around the coffee pot handle. Paul watched apprehensively.

'You aren't going to throw that, are you, darling?'

'If you don't get to the point ... yes!'

'You want the details?' He pretended to be doubtful. 'All the details?'

'Every single damned detail!'

'Well, we danced for a while ...'

'I remember that. Get on with it.'

'I warned you about the retsina, you know. I'm afraid you were too headstrong. You were, to put it politely, just the tiniest bit tight.'

Grimly she nodded. 'That much is obvious.'

'Your legs gave way suddenly and I carried you up to bed. But you were very affectionate.' He gave her one of his sidelong, teasing smiles. 'I must remember that retsina makes you so very warm and loving.'

'Devil!' she exploded. 'So you took advantage of ...'

'Darling girl,' he protested. 'You wouldn't let me go.'

Scarlet, she bit her lip. 'And so?' she asked hoarsely.

'So . . .' his voice was smooth, 'I kissed you and so on.'

'The "and so on" bit interests me,' she said tautly.

He grinned. 'I thought it might.' He laughed. 'Your face! No, Leonie, I did not consummate our marriage last night, tempted though I certainly was by your delightful invitation . . .'

'Why, you . . .' she bit back the words hovering on her tongue. Relief flooded her—relief and a certain secret feeling of pique. He said she had been inviting. Why then had he resisted the invitation? Presumably because he had not wanted her. Well, she was relieved and delighted, of course. Of course . . .

Paul was drinking his coffee. She glanced at him. 'I'm sorry I embarrassed you,' she said tightly. 'Obviously I was too drunk to know what I was doing.'

'You didn't embarrass me,' he said lightly.

'Good of you to say so,' she retorted.

'You were rather sleepy, very friendly and entirely delightful,' he said easily. 'If you want the absolute truth, I would have stayed and made love to you all night if you hadn't fallen asleep about five minutes after I started kissing you.'

'Oh.' Her fingers trembled. 'I fell asleep?'

'Out like a light.' He gave her an amused smile. 'I may say it nearly drove me mad. There you were in my arms, as soft as a kitten, and all I could do was tiptoe away.'

She pushed her coffee cup away with an abrupt motion. 'Paul, this can't go on. It was a mistake to come up here. We're too isolated. We should have gone to Paris, after all.'

'Too late now,' he said lightly.

'We could say we'd changed our minds, take the next plane to Paris.'

'No,' he said, shaking his head. 'It would cause too much comment if we suddenly came back from here. We have to stay for the full week.'

'I can't!' She almost wailed.

'Just stay off the retsina,' he advised gravely.

Leonie gave an outraged gasp and stood up. 'You ... you ... God grant me patience with you!'

'Amen,' he said softly.

She fled from the room in total disarray, and Paul leaned back in his chair and laughed aloud.

CHAPTER FIVE

LEONIE walked slowly through the olive grove, watching the leaves turn restlessly on their branches in a light breeze. The goats were bleating angrily, and she wondered if they needed milking. Yesterday Paul had milked them before waking her, and she had been surprised and impressed by the fact that he knew how to cope with them.

Paul called her from the door of the house, and she went reluctantly back towards him.

'Come and help me with the goats,' he said casually.

'What?' She was aghast.

'They must be frantic,' he explained. 'We can do it twice as fast together.'

'I've never milked a goat in my life!' she protested.

'Time you learnt, then.'

'I don't think I could!' she protested.

'It's easy,' he shrugged. 'I'll teach you.'

It was by no means easy, but after a few false starts she found herself picking up the knack, although the goats were restless and irritable confronted with her novice hands.

'Like most females they recognise a master,' Paul said teasingly.

'They recognise experienced handling, you mean,' she said disgustedly.

He grinned. 'You've a very sharp tongue, Leonie.'

They took the milk into the cold larder at the back of the house. It was built there to be out of the sun, Paul explained. The cold temperature of the night was retained for a long time. The floor of the little room was lower than that of the house, sunk deep into the ground, and the milk was kept down there in the coldest part of the room.

'The man who lives here will come up during the day to take some of the milk and eggs. He makes cheese and sells it. Once a week they sail over to the mainland and dispose of their produce.'

'They must lead very stark lives,' she commented.

'Very contented ones. They have their own land and enough to eat, clothes to wear and money for such things as tools. What more could they need?'

'An easier life,' she suggested.

'What? Television, a car, a washing machine? They are all luxuries designed to make town life less ugly and boring. Country people need them less because the surroundings of their lives are so much more creative. Town life makes you soft. Life out here is tougher, but the people are tougher, too.'

'Yet you prefer town life,' she pointed out drily.

He grinned. 'I'm a hybrid. I can exist out here, believe me. But the so-called civilised world is where I make my money.'

'And where the pretty girls are to be found,' she suggested, tongue in cheek.

'That, too,' he agreed calmly.

They washed, collected some more cold food and set off for another walk.

'Not so far this time,' Paul promised. 'But I want you to see as much of Comus as possible. After all, it is as much your home as ours now.'

They took a gently sloping path round the curve of a hill, meeting a goat boy driving his flock with a short, peeled stick. He smiled at them and Paul stopped to talk to him in quick Greek. The boy glanced at Leonie and said something politely. Paul turned to her and said, 'This is Petros. He asks if you would care for a drink of goats' milk. For God's sake say yes or he'll be very hurt.'

She smiled at the boy. 'Thank you,' she said in Greek, nodding.

Carefully, the boy pulled out a wooden bowl from his rough shirt. He milked one of the goats and offered her the bowl with a little bow.

With gravity, she took it, smiled at him, lifted it to her lips and drained it slowly. She thanked him again in Greek, and his sallow face lit up.

On an impulse, Leonie bent and plucked a sprig of rosemary growing near their path and handed it to Petros, who took it wonderingly, smiled again and pushed the plant into the top of his shirt.

They parted with much smiling and exchange of farewells. Paul looked down at her, his face serious.

'That was a very charming gesture—rosemary for remembrance. Petros will certainly remember meeting you today. He was at our wedding, of course, like the rest of the islanders, and he will be eager to tell everyone how he gave the new Kyria Caprel a drink of his milk and she gave him a flower in exchange.'

She flushed. 'I wanted to give him something without offending him.'

'Your instinct was sound. He was delighted.' Paul took her hand in his, raised it to his lips tenderly, looking into her eyes with a charming, affectionate smile. 'I found the incident very touching. Argon will be very pleased.'

Leonie glanced round and saw Petros watching them from a little hillock. No doubt to him they looked like fond lovers. She gave the boy a little wave, and he at once waved back.

Walking on, Paul asked, 'By the way, how was the goats' milk?'

'Vile,' she grimaced.

He gave a bark of laughter. 'Then you are a better actress than I gave you credit for, because you gave the distinct impression that you found it delicious.'

'I couldn't hurt the boy's feelings.'

'No,' he agreed quickly. 'I'm very grateful to you.'

They came to a little group of laurels half an hour later, and decided to eat their lunch there in the shade.

'I hope you won't get sick of cold lamb,' he commented.

'I'm too hungry to care what I eat,' she told him.

After eating, they lay back in the shade and watched the laurels fluttering faintly in the wind. The sun filtered through the leaves, dappling the ground with a chiaroscuro of light and shade, turning Paul's face into a black-barred mask. Paul sighed.

'We could stay here all afternoon and doze. Or would you rather walk back?'

'I'm quite happy to stay here,' she agreed.

He stretched out his long legs, folding his arms beneath his blond head. 'Good.'

Leonie let her thoughts drift lazily, reviewing the events of the past few days. She wished she could remember all that had happened last night. What exactly had she said or done to make Paul believe she wanted him to stay with her? She shifted restlessly, dwelling on visions of herself begging him to make love to her. Thank God she had fallen asleep! She raised herself a little to look at Paul. He was fast asleep, his fair lashes shadowed on his tanned skin. He looked vulnerable and gentle like this, his mocking mouth still and relaxed, the brilliant blue eyes which could be so insolent and self-assured hidden under their white lids. Deep in the pit of her stomach an ache began and spread up through her body.

Oh, God, she thought despairingly, not that! I couldn't stand falling in love again. I won't expose myself to pain and bitterness again.

But her eyes continued to survey him hungrily, tracing the hard curve of his profile; the faint laughter lines at mouth and eye, the strong jaw and straight nose, the way in which his lashes brushed his cheek, the fine moulding of the cheekbones, the golden hair just visible above his upper lip. The mouth itself fascinated her. It held such conflicting indications: the lower lip had a tight strength which the full, sensual upper lip defied and the shape of it was entirely dictated by the long, powerful jaw, giving it power and charm, a ruthless combination. The attraction of his face was not, she decided, so much in the colouring or shape of the features, but in the underlying bone structure.

His eyes suddenly lifted and looked straight into hers, his blue gaze searching her face intently. She looked away, terrified of revealing how she felt.

'Go to sleep, Leonie,' he said softly, after a long moment.

She lay down and composed herself for sleep, still shaking. But to her surprise she slowly slid into a deep dream-filled sleep. The dreams were all of Paul. Freed from shame or pride, she let herself explore the true depths of her feelings for him, and awoke with a reluctant jolt to find him still sleeping beside her, curled close to her back, one hand flung out towards her waist.

When she sat up he woke, too, yawned and said sleepily, 'Good heavens, look at the time ... we must get back to milk the goats before we eat dinner.'

'Milk them again?' she cried in horror.

He laughed. 'Morning and evening. Didn't you realise?'

'A hotel in Paris looks more and more attractive to me,' she returned lightly.

'I thought you were beginning to enjoy yourself,' he said reproachfully.

She smiled. 'I am! I was only teasing.'

'A dangerous game,' he said lightly, but with a

hidden but pointed meaning.

Leonie felt her cheeks grow pink. They walked back slowly in the cool of the evening. Paul told her old legends of the island, stories of satyrs, nymphs, amorous gods.

'It must be something in the air,' she said.

He grinned. 'More likely the retsina.'

Again she blushed. 'I wish you'd forget that!'

'How could I forget anything so delightful?' His teasing was brotherly, yet an undertone of something more intimate alarmed her.

Together they milked the goats. Their absent host had been to the house during their absence and removed most of the earlier milk and eggs, leaving them sufficient for the next day.

'Thank God for that,' Leonie sighed. 'I was beginning to be afraid we would have to bath in it soon.'

'Now that,' said Paul, 'is a marvellous idea.' He slid a glance over her. 'You're still quite pale in places—not that it shows.'

'I thought I was getting very brown,' she said, looking at her arms and shoulders, which were tanning a lovely golden brown.

'You should have brought your bikini,' Paul suggested. 'Of course, you could always sunbathe in the nude.'

'I wouldn't want to shock Petros,' she returned.

'Never mind Petros,' he said easily.

'I'll make supper,' she said hastily, her pulses fluttering at his glance.

'That's right,' he said drily. 'Run away.'

She ignored that thrust and concentrated on getting the meal. Inevitably, they had rice and salad, but she had found some dolmades in the cold store; meat and herbs wrapped in vine leaves, and they began their meal with these and followed the dolmades with kebabs.

Over coffee Paul suggested that they play cards. 'It will pass the time and save you from the retsina.' They had not drunk wine tonight with their meal. Leonie had not put the bottle on the table, and Paul's wry look had underlined its absence.

They played cards noisily, with childish abandon. To make it more interesting, they played for money; a handful of small change which crossed and re-crossed the table as the tide of battle ebbed and flowed. Paul gradually won it all until Leonie had no change left.

'I'll play you for kisses,' Paul suggested, tongue in cheek.

'No, thank you,' she said with dignity. 'As I've no money I won't play at all.'

'Spoilsport!' he retorted.

'I'll wash up,' she said, rising from the table.

'I'll help you.'

They finished the washing up, then looked at the clock. After her long sleep under the laurels Leonie was not tired. She did not want to go to bed yet, but she was nervous of being alone with Paul, especially as he was in such a teasing mood.

'A moonlight stroll?' Paul suggested.

She regarded him dubiously.

'I promise to be very brotherly,' he murmured.

'I didn't say a word,' she protested.

He moved closer to look down at her, his blue eyes provocative. 'Does that mean I needn't be brotherly?'

'You are the most maddening man!' she burst out.

He grinned. 'That makes us quits, then, because you are enough to drive a saint mad.'

Leonie moved to the door. He followed and they stood outside, surveying the sky for a while. The moon had risen, silvering the olives and softening the barren outlines of the hills. The landscape had a timeless grandeur. Leonie felt a moved affinity with it, tracing the stark peaks with a loving eye.

It was much cooler now that the sun had gone down. A wind was blowing in from the sea, driving the laurels and olives into a twisting dance. A cypress tree on the edge of the olive grove blew wildly, bending almost double, its flame-shaped trunk springing back to cut a black outline against the sky.

They walked towards the olive grove in silence. Leonie was enjoying the feel of the wind along her arms, its ruffling fingers in her hair, when suddenly she tripped over a stone and fell clumsily.

Paul exclaimed and knelt beside her, lifting her. 'Are you hurt?'

'My ankle,' she breathed on a gasp of pain.

His fingers felt along her leg. She repressed a groan as he touched the painful swelling over her ankle.

'Sprained, I think,' he said gently. 'Poor girl, what

a thing to happen!' He hesitated, then said, 'Shall I try to carry you? If it hurts too much, yell.'

He lifted her tentatively, avoiding touching her ankle. 'There. All right?'

'Yes,' she whispered huskily, her energy concentrated on fighting down pain.

He carried her back to the house, where he bathed her ankle with ice-cold water from the stream and wrapped it in bandages. Then he gave her a strong glass of local brandy and carried her up to bed.

'This is becoming quite a habit,' he said as he laid her on her bed.

'I'm sorry,' she muttered.

'I enjoy it,' he returned. 'I'll help you undress.'

'I can do it,' she said quickly. 'I've hurt my foot, not my hand.'

'I've seen you undressed before,' he pointed out.

She flushed. 'Please, Paul ... leave me alone now...'

He looked down at her, his expression wry. 'You realise that you've won?'

'Won?' She was bewildered.

'We'll have to leave now. Even Argon will realise that a badly sprained ankle is a good enough excuse for ending a honeymoon in a remote hill cottage.'

'Oh!' She flushed again. It had not occurred to her, and now that it did she was forced to admit to herself that she was not very pleased with the idea. 'But I could never walk down to the road,' she protested. 'How would we get back?'

'That's easy,' he shrugged. 'I'll borrow a donkey for you from our neighbours.'

'Neighbours?' She was puzzled. 'What neighbours?'

'Petros and his family live just a few miles over the second hill,' he said.

'But that's a long walk!'

'You won't be afraid if I leave you alone at night? I'll go now and be back by morning.'

'You can't walk that far at this time of night!'

'Far less tiring than walking in daylight,' he said. 'It's so much cooler.'

'Oh, but ...' She bit her lip.

He looked at her gently. 'There's no need to be afraid. There's no one on this island who would harm you. You'll be quite safe.'

Then he was gone and Leonie was alone in the circle of yellow light thrown by the candle. She felt bitter tears rise to her eyes. Their days of isolation were over. They would be leaving this little house tomorrow, and she knew she hated the thought of leaving. She had been desperately happy here today, looking forward to the other days with a sort of nervous, hopeful anticipation. She clumsily undressed and fell into bed, only to lie awake for hours listening to the owls making their melancholy sound in the olive grove.

Paul woke her up at dawn with a cup of coffee and a slice of toasted pitta. 'I've got two donkeys,' he told her. 'I'll bind your ankle carefully before we start. I think you should make it without much trouble.'

She dressed with great difficulty and hopped down the stairs. Paul turned in surprise. 'You should have waited until I carried you down,' he protested. 'How's the ankle?'

'Not too bad,' she lied.

He knelt and unwound the bandages, wincing at the swollen blue and purple lump on her foot. 'Not bad? It looks ghastly,' he said. 'It must hurt like hell.'

He bathed it in cold water again and re-bandaged it. Then he left her to drink some more coffee while he packed everything. Half an hour later they were on their way.

Leonie soon accustomed herself to the jogging of the donkey. Now and then she forgot to protect her ankle from bumping against something, then she had to bite her lip to silence a cry of pain. Paul was watching her all the time, his gaze sober. She knew he was anxious about her and it touched her.

They reached the road and found the silver grey limousine waiting for them. She gave an exclamation of astonishment, and Paul smiled at her.

'Petros insisted on going off to tell Argon the news,' he informed her. 'I guessed he would send the car to pick us up.'

It was only a short while later that they were safely back at Argon's villa, and Leonie was being protectively tucked up in bed by Clyte.

Argon was furious with Paul. 'You were very careless with Leonie! This is all your fault!'

Paul looked sombre. 'How could I foresee that she would trip over in the moonlight?'

Argon's eyes narrowed. 'In the moonlight, eh? And what were you doing ... in the moonlight?'

'Taking a stroll before bed,' Paul said curtly.

Argon made a sound of disgust. 'If you had taken her to bed instead of taking her for a stroll this would not have happened! I thought you were supposed to be such a man of the world! Is this how you court a girl? Trip her up like a caveman and maim her?'

'Oh, God help us!' Paul muttered furiously.

'Don't you swear at me, you spawn of Satan,' Argon scolded him.

'I should have done what my instincts told me was best and taken her to Paris,' Paul said bitterly. 'And that's just what I shall do now.'

'Paris,' said Argon doubtfully.

'World-renowned as a honeymoon city,' Paul told him with a sardonic smile.

'I don't like it,' Argon pronounced.

'I'm not asking you to come,' said Paul.

Argon muttered ferociously and gave up the struggle.

Next day, while Clyte packed her clothes, Argon talked to Leonie gently, trying to discover the exact state of her feelings, but failing.

She was determined to conceal from him both her own feelings for Paul and just how badly the first few days of their honeymoon had gone. Argon left her feeling unsatisfied. A further interview with Paul left him no wiser, but he was not altogether unhopeful. They might not know it, but there was a visible tension between them whenever they were together, and on this sign of awareness Argon placed all his hopes for their future.

They flew to Paris next morning. Leonie was feeling rather tired. She had not been able to sleep since returning from the hills; her ankle kept her awake. During the slow progress of the hours she had plenty of time to think about herself and Paul. She had admitted to herself now that she was madly in love with him. She had been preconditioned to fall for him by her schoolhood obsession about him. That charming, romantic image had sunk deep into her subconscious. No wonder that faced with the real man she had been swept off her feet. Paul's attraction towards herself was something which she could not quite decide upon. From his past record, he would have made a pass at any pretty girl into whose company he was exclusively thrown. That he liked her, even desired her, she was fairly sure; there had been nothing fake about the way he made love. But she was just one of a long procession of dazzling girls who had passed through his life. She had never fancied joining a queue, and she did not intend to do so now.

Paul must never suspect that her feelings for him were any deeper than his feelings for her. She had already betrayed herself sufficiently for him to be aware that he attracted her physically.

She would allow him to go on thinking it a mere physical attraction. It would flatter his vanity, of course, but that was better than letting him know she loved him. No doubt countless women had found him physically attractive. Paul appeared to prefer such uncomplicated relationships. Real emotion made one too vulnerable, perhaps, or was it that he was too self-contained, too downright selfish, to fall in love? Whatever the reason, he must not know, or even suspect, that she was in love with him. He would only despise her, or pity, or both, and she could not bear either.

Paul's flat was in a quiet residential street in a fashionable quarter. Elegantly if impersonally furnished, it had three large bedrooms, two reception rooms and a luxuriously fitted kitchen and bathroom.

'Choose which bedroom you like,' Paul told her.

'Which is yours?' she asked.

He looked at her from beneath his lashes. 'Whichever you please.'

She sighed. 'Which one was yours?'

He grinned, indicating a door. Leonie promptly opened the second door along. The room revealed was large, sunny and comfortable.

'I'll have this one,' she told him. He carried her luggage into the room, then suggested she rest before dinner. They had eaten lunch on the plane, the usual cardboard meal, satisfying neither appetite nor senses.

'Will we eat here?' she asked.

'I'll have a meal sent in,' he suggested. 'What would you like? Chinese? Indian? Greek?'

'Chinese, I think,' she murmured.

He nodded. 'Fine. Now, try to sleep. You're quite white, you know. The journey was exhausting for you.'

She was glad to fall in with his plans, and managed to sleep for a few hours, until he woke her to eat their evening meal. She had time to wash and change before the delivery man rang the door bell and wheeled in a trolley laden with steaming food. Paul paid him, unloaded the dishes and saw him back to the door with his trolley.

She peeped into the foil dishes. 'Mm ... sweetcorn and chicken soup, prawn crackers, sweet and sour king prawn, beef and noodles, egg foo young...' She grinned at Paul. 'I'm starving!'

'I hoped you would like what I ordered. I probably got too much, but I had to guess at what you would like, so I ordered more dishes to give us a wider choice.'

'Makes a change from goats' cheese and pitta,' she teased.

'I rather like goats' cheese and pitta,' he said solemnly.

She laughed. 'So do I, actually. Or I was just getting to like it. I've discovered that when you're hungry you will eat almost anything edible.'

'The same has been said about women,' Paul retorted.

Leonie went white.

He looked quickly at her, his eyes shocked. 'My dear girl, I meant nothing personal. That wasn't aimed at you. It was just a cheap joke...'

'Yes, it was,' she said bitterly. 'True, all the same, isn't it? Don't they say that all cats are grey in the night?'

'Cynicism doesn't become you,' he said fiercely.

'Have I shocked you? I'm sorry. Obviously I've been influenced by the last few days I've spent with you.' Her voice was tinged with sardonic mockery.

'I don't like to hear you talk like that! You're too young to understand what cynicism does to one. It's like a grey mist covering everything beautiful.' His tone hardened, the blue eyes angry. 'When you are young you admire cynics. You should pity them. They have lost their natural love of life.'

'You should know,' she said quietly.

Paul's lips tightened. 'Yes.' He gestured to the dining table. 'Shall we eat? This food is getting cold.'

Leonie regretted having spoilt their mood. It happened every time. They would reach a point of contact only to have the moment shattered by a remark one or other of them made. Their relationship was as brittle as glass. One false move and it cracked wide open.

CHAPTER SIX

Next morning Leonie woke up with a strange sense of confusion, and lay for a moment trying to re-orientate herself. She realised at last that she had grown unaccustomed to the sound of traffic outside her window in the mornings. It had been so quiet on Comus. Only the slow swell of the waves and the weird cries of seagulls ever disturbed the peace there. Paris traffic, too, was much noisier than the English variety. In London it was illegal to blare one's car-horn quite so frequently, and car drivers only hooted when it was strictly necessary, either in warning or in real anger. But here in Paris the constant hooting of horns and the squeal of brakes made the early morning unbearable.

Leonie slid out of bed and padded barefoot to the window. The pale yellow velvet curtains slid apart at a touch and daylight dazzled her eyes. When she grew used to the light she stared out at the street, admiring the elegant architecture of the nineteenth-century houses.

After a few moments she moved across the room and put on her dressing-gown, then went out to the kitchen to make a pot of tea. The room was ex-pensively equipped and packed with labour-saving gadgets, and it would, she thought, be a pleasure to work in it. While the kettle was boiling she hunted through the cupboards and discovered the various ingredients for breakfast.

Ten minutes later she took a cup of tea in to Paul. He was asleep, his sheets flung back in disorder.

She put the cup down and turned to wake him, only to find him stirring. He smiled at her, his eyes half-closed. 'Tea? Thank you. You're up early. Couldn't sleep?'

'I slept very well. What do you want for breakfast?'

He made a face. 'I'm not very hungry. Some fruit, I think. I'll get up in a moment.'

'I can find everything I need, don't worry,' she said, leaving the room.

She found some breakfast cereal and sat down to eat it at the kitchen table. Suddenly she heard a footstep in the hall, and went out to find a strange man standing there. Dark-suited, dark-haired and elegant, he looked casually at home and seemed amused to see her.

His brows rose. 'Good morning! So Paul is home, is he?'

'Yes,' she said uncertainly. Who on earth was he? And how had he got into the flat?

His cool grey eyes skimmed her appreciatively. 'May I say how much I admire Paul's taste, as always?'

She felt her cheeks flush. He thought ... that she was one of Paul's lady-friends! 'Thank you,' she said stiffly.

The other man looked even more amused by her reaction. 'Where is Paul? Not still in bed?'

'Yes,' she said coldly. 'I'll tell him we have a visitor. Who shall I say it is?'

'I'll go straight in, thanks,' the man replied, turning to the door of Paul's room.

Feeling like stamping her foot, Leonie returned to the kitchen and got on with her breakfast. She had finished it and was washing up at the sink when the kitchen door opened to admit the visitor. He looked gravely at her.

'Paul has told me what a fool I made of myself. I beg your pardon, Mrs Caprel. I leapt to unwarrantable conclusions. I hope you can forgive me?'

'You said nothing out of place,' she said coolly, picking up a dish cloth.

'My manner was over-familiar,' he returned. 'Permit me to do penance by drying up for you.' He moved over and took the cloth from her hand, smiling down at her with warm charm. 'I must have given you a shock, materialising like that. While Paul was away I had the key to this flat. I sometimes borrow it for a day or two while I'm in Paris. I run the London end of Paul's business, you see, but I am often over here in France and it saves on hotel bills if I stay here.'

'I can see it would,' she said drily.

The grey eyes flicked to her thoughtfully. 'My name, by the way, is Jake Tennyson. I've known Paul for ten years. We are old friends as well as business partners.'

She nodded. 'So I gathered.'

He made a wry face. 'I hope I let no cats out of any bags?'

The phrase made her laugh. 'I don't think you told me anything I didn't know.'

'I'm fond of Paul,' he said casually. 'I would hate to make waves for him.'

'Don't worry,' she assured him. 'There will be no waves.'

He smiled suddenly, his lean dark face lightening. 'I'm very relieved to hear that. Paul is a lucky fellow.'

The kitchen door opened at that moment, and Paul shot into the room. He looked as if he had thrown his clothes on in a hurry. The blue eyes moved from one to the other of them, taking in the dishcloth in Jake's hand and Leonie's flushed face.

His brows jerked together.

'I gather you've introduced yourself.'

Jake nodded. 'Paul, you always did have the devil's own luck. This girl is one in a million.'

Paul hardly looked flattered. He nodded without replying, then said, 'Come through into the sitting-room, Jake. We'll talk business in there. No doubt Leonie has a dozen things she wants to do.' His blue eyes shot coldly at her. 'Including getting dressed.' And he glanced meaningly at the flimsy cotton dressing-gown she wore.

She flushed, clutching the open neck of the dressing-gown with one hand, only now realising that it revealed rather a lot of her throat and shoulders, and that the brief nightie she wore was even more revealing.

'Leonie,' Jake murmured softly. 'What a delightful and unusual name. It suits you.' The grey eyes touched on her hand, holding the neckline of her dressing-gown together. A shrewd glint came into them as he glanced back at Paul.

Paul indicated the door, his face openly grim. Jake followed him out of the room. As the door swung closed, Leonie heard his voice.

'So you finally got caught in the trap, Paul.'

Paul's reply was inaudible, but the tone in which it was uttered was curt and angry. Did Paul resent their marriage? she wondered unhappily. Did he feel trapped?

She went back to her bedroom and hunted out a dress to wear. Her ankle was still sore, but she was able to hobble about quite deftly now. So long as she did not put any weight on the swollen ankle, she could move about quite freely.

Dressed and made up, she returned to the kitchen to make herself a cup of coffee. She needed to think.

She had returned here with Paul, but since their marriage was to be purely platonic, she saw no real reason why she should stay with him. Her job was waiting for her in London. She had written to her boss to tell him that she was getting married, and he had replied that he hoped she would be happy, but that if ever she needed a job she was to write to him. There was no reason why she should not take up her life where she had left off—no reason she was prepared to admit, anyway.

Paul joined her a few moments later. He was alone, and Leonie looked at him in surprise. 'Where's Jake?' she asked.

'You got on first name terms pretty quickly,' Paul said with cold displeasure.

'Did you want me to call him Mr Tennyson?' She pretended innocence.

'I want you to keep out of Jake's way in future,' Paul said grimly. 'He's a notorious wolf, and you, my dear, are just the type of little lamb to appeal to him.'

'I will not be dictated to,' she said in determined tones. 'I think we must get a few things straight here and now. When we made our bargain nothing was said about your having the right to tell me which friends to choose or how to behave. We are legally man and wife, but it stops there. I intend to remain a free agent, doing just as I please.'

'Do you indeed?' he bit out sharply.

'Yes,' her chin was lifted in defiance, her eyes flashed across the room at him. 'You have no rights where I'm concerned, Paul, none at all.'

'Not even the right to expect you to make Argon happy by keeping up appearances?' he asked sarcastically.

She hesitated, frowning.

He went on coldly, 'If you were seen with Jake in public how long do you think it would take the gossip hounds to put two and two together? Our marriage must already have aroused suspicions of an arranged match. They'll all be watching closely to see whether their suspicions are correct. Such speculation would upset Argon a great deal.'

'But he knows perfectly well that our marriage is one of pure convenience,' she protested.

'Of course he does, but he still expects us to keep up a public façade convincing enough to persuade everyone else that our marriage is a normal one in every respect. You can't afford to be seen with other men in public, you can't allow anyone to suspect that you're not the radiant young bride you ought to be so soon after your marriage.'

She flushed at the sardonic note in his voice. 'Are you trying to make me a sort of prisoner, Paul?'

'No, of course not, but you are my wife, whether you like it or not.' He turned away, driving his hands into his pockets and hunching his shoulders irritably. 'Whether I like it or not,' he added in a fierce mutter.

Leonie felt a quick sting of pain. She foresaw how bitter an experience it would be to pretend to be a happily married woman while constantly aware of Paul's resentment.

'Very well,' she said. 'What do you expect me to do?'

'Now that we're back in Paris my friends will expect us to entertain. They'll want to meet you. I'll give you a list of names. We'll hold a series of dinner parties so that you can get to know them all.' He turned to study her coolly. 'You will need new clothes, too. You always look very pretty, but you must realise that as my wife you will be expected to dress superbly. I'll take you to Thérèse, I think.'

'Thérèse?' she asked blankly. One of his girl-friends? she wondered.

He smiled suddenly. 'You'll like her, I think. She's an original and she creates clothes that bear an unmistakable hallmark. She'll find the right style for your looks.'

They drove to the salon that afternoon. It was situated in a wide, traffic-crowded avenue. A shining expanse of plate glass gilded with the name Thérèse slid open as they approached with the noiseless efficiency of expensive electronics, and they found themselves in a white-carpeted lounge some thirty feet long. A few deep-cushioned chairs stood about the room. Behind a desk sat a long-legged dark girl with sleek hair and an enamelled beauty which was matched by the superb cut of the black dress she wore. She looked at them calmly, a faint smile on her red mouth.

'M'sieur Paul,' she lisped softly, rising. 'Madame is expecting you. Will you go through?' Her dark eyes surveyed Leonie with hard curiosity.

Paul put a hand beneath Leonie's elbow and guided her across the white carpet to a discreet little door at the side with the word *Directrice* printed on it.

He tapped, then pushed the door open. From a large leather desk piled high with papers arose a tiny, white-haired woman who gave a deep-throated murmur of welcome.

'Paul, *mon cher* ... there you are!' She darted across the room and kissed him on both cheeks, reaching up on her toes to do so, her hands holding his shoulders. 'You look very brown. How was Comus? Ah, I envy you that little retreat! The world is too much with us here in Paris.' On the words she turned to study Leonie with direct and unblinking curiosity. She had a withered complexion, the wrinkled olive skin of a tortoise, her mouth wide and passionate, her nose as sharp as a knife, fleshless and dominant. It was a striking face, but the black eyes gave it such life that at first one noticed nothing else.

'So...' The quick, deep voice held a note of satisfaction. 'So this is your wife. *Bon.*' A smile lit her face and she held out her hands to Leonie. 'I am very happy to meet you, *ma petite.*'

Leonie murmured a polite response, observing as she did so that Thérèse was wearing a dress cut on austere but impeccable lines. Her eyes met those of the older woman as each surveyed the other carefully.

'Madame, I want you to design Leonie a new wardrobe,' Paul told her. 'A look created especially for her.'

A small, thin hand caught Leonie's chin between claw-like fingers and turned her face this way and that while the dark eyes continued to inspect her.

'What a bone structure! It will be a pleasure, Paul, to create clothes for her. She is Greek, of course. One sees the eyes, the skin ... what else could she be? Such lustrous hair ... a healthy texture, unmistakable shine.' An approving smile was conferred upon Leonie. '*Bien.* First, we take your measurements. Then you go away. I do some sketches, then you return and see what I have done. If you approve, I will have some of the clothes made up. Then we have the fittings.' The black eyes twinkled. 'It takes time, you see?'

'But it is well worth waiting for,' Paul drawled.

The old woman laughed. 'I am glad you think so,

Paul. Young people are so impatient these days. Instant everything ... coffee, food, clothes. They hate to wait, even for the best, but for the best one always has to wait ...'

Turning away she pressed a bell. The door opened and a plump, smiling woman appeared. Madame indicated Leonie.

'Take Madame Caprel and measure her, Ariette.'

The other woman nodded, smiled at Leonie and gestured to the door. 'If you will follow me, Madame?'

Leonie found herself in a small cubicle lined with mirrors. The carpets were thick and luxurious, discreet lighting gave the room an air of romance which the faint scent lingering on the air emphasised.

Patiently Leonie stood very still while the other woman took careful measurements, noting them down in a small notebook. Even her wrists were measured, to Leonie's amusement.

Returning to the office, Ariette handed Madame Thérèse the notebook, then left. Thérèse glanced down the page, smiled and put the book away.

'I have discovered from your husband what sort of clothes you will need,' she said in satisfaction. 'Now will you take tea with me?'

'That would be very pleasant, Madame, but unhappily we have too many other things to do this afternoon,' Paul said. 'Another time, perhaps?'

They drove back to the flat and found a letter on the doormat. Paul slit it open and read it, his face oddly blank, while Leonie waited for him to tell her

what they were going to do for the rest of the day.
She felt restless, uneasy. She had no roots here in
Paris. She had no friends, no occupation. The future
stretched ahead of her, as blank and mysterious as a
dream forgotten on waking.

Paul looked up. 'We have an invitation,' he said
slowly.

Her mind leapt to the obvious. 'From Jake?'

Paul frowned. 'No, not from Jake,' he said coldly.
'From Diane Irvine, an old friend of mine.'

An old girl-friend? Leonie knew that she would
never find out from Paul's face. He was too good at
disguising his thoughts. The handsome features
could assume a masklike impenetrability when he
chose.

'An invitation to what?' she asked.

'Dinner,' he said lightly.

'When?'

'Tonight,' he returned.

She looked horrified. 'But I have nothing to
wear!'

'That can be put right immediately,' he said.
'We'll go out now and buy you a simple little black
dress.'

She was reluctant to meet his friends so soon.
'Must we?' she asked nervously. 'Can't we wait a
while? Until Madame Thérèse has made some
clothes for me?'

Paul looked at her coolly. 'I want you to go
tonight,' he said flatly. 'Diane has invited six of my
best friends, and it will be an ideal opportunity to
introduce you to them all. Now that you've met Jake

there's no hope of fending off the rest of them. It's a pity Jake happened to arrive today, but it's done now. The whole of Paris will know we're back by tomorrow and the telephone will never stop ringing. We must face the inevitable.'

Leonie sighed. 'Very well.' Glancing at him, she asked, 'Is Diane married?'

'Yes,' he said curtly.

'What does her husband do?'

'He's a merchant banker,' said Paul. 'I think you'll like him. He's a very likeable man.'

'Irvine is an English name,' she said thoughtfully.

'George is an Englishman,' Paul stated. 'His wife is French, however. George runs the French end of his bank. Although he's English, he was born in Switzerland, and he spends a lot of time in Geneva, but Diane is usually in Paris. She hates to leave the city. She's a sophisticated city-dweller. All her pleasures are to be found here. She detests the country, but George has a passion for English country houses which he never gets the chance to enjoy because Diane would never consent to living over there.'

'Poor George,' said Leonie sympathetically.

Paul's mouth twisted ironically. 'I knew you would sympathise with him.'

They went out and chose a dress at an expensive boutique. Paul insisted on making the final decision. His taste, Leonie realised, ran to clothes of stylish simplicity, and she had to admit that the dress he chose suited her.

When she was dressed that evening, Paul surveyed

her from head to toe, his eyes narrowed. 'Yes,' he said at last, 'you'll do. But there's one thing missing...' He produced a flat jeweller's box. Flapping it open, he drew out a diamond and emerald necklace. Leonie gasped.

'Paul! I was going to wear the jewels Argon gave me!'

'I want you to wear these,' he said offhandedly, walking round behind her to clasp them. She quivered at the touch of his cool fingers on her skin. It took him some time to manipulate the clasp and her nerves were stretched intolerably when he at last moved away.

'Thank you,' she said, touching the cold gems with one finger. 'It was very kind of you.'

He shrugged. 'I want you to look like my wife,' he said in a tight voice.

'Of course,' she said, her voice faint. The necklace was window-dressing for the benefit of his friends who must not suspect that their marriage was merely in name only.

They arrived at Diane Irvine's beautiful Napoleonic house just after eight. A wall surrounded the courtyard in which the house stood. A line of bay trees in green tubs lined the path to the front door, and the façade was lit by coach lamps hanging from pedestals outside the porch.

Paul seized the brass knocker and banged it once. A moment later the door flew open and a tall, elegantly gowned woman stood there facing them.

'Paul, *mon cher! Ça va, mon vieux?* You were so sly to get married far away on your Greek island

where none of us could get a glimpse of your bride!'
The soft, smiling voice included them both in these
remarks, but Leonie realised that the bright blue
eyes which studied her held no smile. Beneath their
hard shine lay a nameless hostility.

Diane Irvine was in her late twenties, Leonie
judged. The blonde hair was styled in apparently
casual curls and hung to her shoulders. Her skin had
a peachy bloom. Her figure was rounded, curved in
the right places with a ripeness which just missed
being overblown. The turquoise dress she wore was
cleverly cut to add height and make her look slim-
mer.

Paul murmured an introduction, and Diane ex-
tended a languid hand. Leonie met it with her own
and they smiled at each other, the smiles which
society imposes for the sake of courtesy but which
are quite meaningless, and serve only to highlight the
false friendliness being offered.

'I did not even know Paul had a cousin Leonie,'
Diane purred, giving him an intimate glance.

'Leonie has been brought up in England,' Paul
explained.

'Poor girl,' smiled Diane. 'I have friends over
there, of course, but I dislike the country. Too cold,
too dull.' The blue eyes narrowed. 'Perhaps you
know some of my friends? The Earl of...'

Leonie broke in swiftly, her voice chilly. 'I don't
know anyone in England whom you would know,
Madame Irvine.' It was not quite true. She had met
many girls at school who came from just such
backgrounds, but she had made few friends among

them, and had not bothered to keep up the acquain-
tance after she left school.

Diane's brows rose. A gleam of triumph shone in
her eyes. 'Oh! My dear, I hope you are not upset by
my question. I naturally thought...' She let her
voice trail away, shrugging in a pretence of helpless-
ness. 'You are a Caprel?' The question was half
statement, gently malicious.

Paul looked grim. 'Surely we are not the first to
arrive, Diane?' he asked coldly.

She gave a tinkling little laugh. 'Oh, no, they are
all here, waiting with bated breath to see what sort
of girl has finally managed to snare Paul Caprel.
Come along!'

As they passed into the hall, with its gilt Empire
mirrors and silky wallpaper, a maid in a black dress
and lace apron hovered to take Leonie's small fur
wrap, a present from Paul that afternoon. Paul and
Diane moved on without Leonie, Diane's hand pos-
sessively curled around Paul's arm, her blonde head
dropping towards his, her voice hushed to inaudi-
bility. Leonie noted the way those long, red-tipped
fingers clung to his dark sleeve, the moist full bloom
of the red mouth as it parted to breathe some word.

There was by now no doubt in her mind that
Diane and Paul had at some time been very close, or
that Diane was still interested in him. Her every look
declared it.

The room into which they now moved was large,
high-ceilinged and beautifully furnished in the Empire style which was most appropriate for a house of
the Napoleonic period. The silk-upholstered chairs

and sofas were in a soft mint green, their legs carved
with elaborate Egyptian-style decorations; sphinx
bodies formed the feet, coiled serpents writhing
along the uprights. On the walls hung two large
paintings of the same period, by some lesser known
artist, and one very large gilded mirror whose four
corners were formed of the heads of Egyptian gods.
Leonie recognised the head of Horus, the hawk god.
The peculiar mixture of silken elegance and barbaric
splendour gave the salon a startling originality.

At first glance the room seemed crowded, but as
Diane began to guide her around, introducing her,
she began to realise that there were, in fact, only
seven new faces for her to identify.

'This is my husband, my dear. George, are you
awake?' Diane used a light, ultra-sweet voice as she
spoke, but the look in the blue eyes was acid. She
gave Leonie a little smile as she added, 'Poor
George, his work is so dull that he is often half
asleep by the time he gets home. I sometimes feel I
have married a dormouse instead of a man!'

George Irvine did not seem abashed or annoyed
by these remarks. He had risen, stocky and already
beginning to lose his mouse-brown hair, and was
offering Leonie his broad, well-shaped hand together
with a sweet, apologetic smile. 'I'm very happy to
meet you, Mrs Caprel,' he said gently.

Someone laughed, smothering the sound with a
gasp. Diane shot a poisonous glance at the others in
the room.

'These two young things are Emilie and Klaus

Schneider,' she said, her blue eyes resting coldly on Emilie.

Klaus Schneider was a very tall, very thin young man of about twenty-five with fine fair hair and grey eyes which remained expressionless even while he bent over Leonie's hand to kiss it. His wife was tiny, her hair bubbling over her head in soft brown curls, her eyes merry and friendly. It was she who had laughed.

'Klaus is in banking,' Diane told Leonie. 'Emilie is ... well, what do you do with yourself all day, Emilie, my dearest? Sew a fine seam?'

Emilie flushed and made no answer. Klaus looked as enigmatic as ever, but Leonie had a faint quiver of intuition as she met his grey eyes. She suspected that Diane's spitefulness towards his wife did not pass him by, and that Klaus resented it deeply, however little he showed it.

She barely had time to exchange a comforting smile with Emilie before Diane had whisked her on to the second couple, who had risen from a sofa to shake hands.

'Two of our American friends,' said Diane. 'Doris and Carl Nieman. They're from Chicago.' The sentence sounded like an accusation, unsoftened by a smile.

Doris was elaborately coiffured and dressed, her birdlike slenderness enhanced by green silk which clung where it touched. The bright brown eyes held warmth and the handshake confirmed it. Leonie felt immediate rapport with her. Carl Nieman was in middle age, his wide shoulders and slim waist demonstrating a physical fitness which did him credit. He, too, grinned with real friendliness as he shook hands.

'So you're the girl Paul finally picked! Well, I hand it to him. He's some picker!'

'Now, don't start giving away too many of my secrets,' Paul said lightly. 'We're still in the honeymoon stage, remember. Leonie has yet to discover much about my wicked past.'

Carl studied Leonie's face with narrowed eyes. 'I guess you needn't worry, Paul. Your wife looks like a mature personality to me. She'll take any dreadful revelations in her stride.'

'Thanks for the vote of confidence,' Leonie said, smiling at him.

Diane waved a hand at the third couple. 'Jean-Claud and Anna St Just—sister and brother, not husband and wife, by the way.'

Jean-Claud was a wiry, vibrant young man with black hair, black eyes, a deeply tanned olive skin and flashing white teeth which he revealed as he smiled at her and murmured a greeting. 'We have all been consumed with curiosity to see you since we heard of Paul's marriage. At first, we could not believe our ears, you understand. It was so sudden, so unexpected! But now, meeting you, I understand very well.' His slanting dark eyes, faun-like under their thin brows, flattered her.

She laughed. 'Thank you, that was a very nice compliment.'

His sister was a quiet, dark girl with her brother's

colouring but none of his personality. She said nothing as she shook hands, merely smiling, with a reserve in her face which was not unfriendly but coolly withdrawn. She was, Leonie guessed, the sort of person who does not jump into friendship but waits cautiously before committing herself.

'A drink before dinner,' George Irvine invited, indicating the collection of decanters and bottles on an occasional table. 'What about you, Madame Caprel? Sherry? Sweet or dry?'

She accepted a glass and said 'Please, do call me Leonie ... everyone...' turning to include the rest of the guests in the plea.

'An enchanting name,' Jean-Claud said enthusiastically.

'Thank you.'

The door opened and the maid appeared, announcing quietly, 'Monsieur Tennyson...'

Paul swung on his heel to face the door, his face hardening in anger. Watching him, Leonie saw his eyes flash in narrowed accusation at Diane, saw her blue eyes shine back at him in pretended innocence.

'Jake, darling!' Diane advanced to kiss the newcomer, smiling sweetly.

Jake looked at her with a grin of indulgent amusement. 'Diane. How kind of you to invite me.' He glanced at Paul over her shoulder. 'Surprised to see me, Paul?'

'Very,' said Paul coldly. 'I thought you had left for London by the afternoon flight—as I suggested.' The words were uttered deliberately, their menace unconcealed.

'Diane persuaded me to stay,' said Jake, his smile growing mocking. 'She wanted me to be here for the party.'

The two men visibly crossed swords. Jake lounged easily, his bearing impressively unaffected by Paul's naked hostility. The other guests were looking faintly puzzled, faintly alarmed.

Paul stared at Diane. 'Wasn't that thoughtful of her?' His tone was barbed.

She hooked a hand through Jake's arm and drew him towards Leonie. 'But of course you are the only one of us who has met Leonie before, aren't you, Jake?' Her laughter was soft. 'Do you know,' she added, half turning towards the others, 'Jake actually mistook Leonie for one of Paul's little dolly birds? He went to the flat and found a pretty girl *en déshabille*, so naturally leapt to the obvious conclusion.' Her smile slid back to Jake. 'Jake was so struck by her that he was wondering how long it would take him to steal her from Paul, only to find, poor Jake, that Paul had actually married this one!'

Hot-cheeked, Leonie turned away blindly towards the door, blundering into Paul's shoulder. He caught her, his arm clasping her around the shoulders. Above her head his voice said icily, 'We all make mistakes, Diane. Some worse than others.' The tone was full of tightly reined fury.

George Irvine slowly stood up. 'Time we went in to dinner,' he said in his calm English voice. 'My dear, your arm...' He firmly took hold of Diane and walked away with her to the door. The other guests followed like sheep. Soon only Paul and

Leonie remained, facing Jake.

'So Diane finally went too far,' Jake said lightly. He shrugged. 'D'you want me to leave, Paul?'

'You had no business repeating that story to Diane,' Paul said. 'You have embarrassed my wife and exposed her to Diane's spite.'

'I apologise, Leonie,' Jake said very gently, looking at Leonie with a serious expression. 'I didn't intend to hurt you, believe me.'

'What did you intend?' Paul demanded. 'You knew that Diane would repeat that story to half Paris. Telling her was telling the world.'

'You were damned rude to me,' Jake said bluntly. 'I suppose I was furious. You practically threw me out as if I were a door-to-door salesman, and I resented it.'

George appeared in the doorway, looking at them soberly. 'We're waiting for you, Paul.'

Jake shrugged, his eyes still engaged in a duel with Paul. 'I'm leaving, George. Make my adieux, will you?'

'You're not leaving,' George said decisively. 'My wife invited you to dinner and you'll stay.'

Paul looked at him, narrow-eyed.

George returned the stare calmly. 'My dear Paul, there'll be enough gossip as it is—if Jake leaves now it will be ten times worse. You have no choice but to keep up appearances. Jake will dine with us and you will behave towards him with the same courtesy you will show all my other guests. For your wife's sake.'

Paul's mouth set grimly. 'Yes, you're right. I wasn't thinking straight.' He glanced at Jake. 'I apologise for my behaviour this morning.'

Jake nodded casually. 'Forget it. It's all been a storm in a tea-cup.' He glanced at George. 'Deliberately blown up, if you'll forgive me, George, by your beautiful wife. Women can be the very devil.'

George did not reply. He turned away and they followed him into the dining-room.

The meal was beautifully cooked and beautifully served. Leaning back in a carved wooden chair, Leonie watched across the white damask cloth as Diane flirted with Jean-Claud, the pure smooth curve of her breasts rising from her gown as she laughed, her skin made almost translucent by the candlelight. A blaze of silver and glass, the soft-footed efficiency of the servants, the dark green velvet of the curtains picked out by a green T'ang horse rearing delicately on a small white shelf in a corner—the room held a discreet elegance Leonie had never experienced before.

Yet beneath all this beauty she felt a coldness which emanated from her hostess. Everything had been chosen to offset Diane's own beauty, not for its own sake, and the general effect was to make one conscious of Diane's icy self-love. Self-centred people chill those who come near them, and Diane had that effect on Leonie. It was not merely that Diane had been malicious towards her. It was Diane's eternal consciousness of self, the deliberate fall of her silky hair as she smiled sidelong, the movement of arm or shoulder, the soft, spiteful remarks which fell from her red mouth.

Emilie sat opposite Leonie and talked to her chattily throughout the meal. They took to each other immediately and were soon fast friends. Emilie confided, as they left the table later, that she, too, had been a target for Diane's spite. 'She hates her bachelor friends to marry and always loathes their wives. Diane likes to have a circle of men friends who adore her. When she was first married she had dozens, but as time goes by they vanish one by one, and Diane is getting desperate.' Emilie's bright eyes danced. 'Time is on our side, you see!'

So it was not only Paul whom Diane regarded jealously as a possession, thought Leonie, relieved. Her expression gave her away. Emilie giggled and whispered to her. 'Diane thought Paul was sure to stay a bachelor, and she was furious when the news broke that he had married you.' Her glance was faintly anxious. 'You will be careful, won't you? She can be very devious and very malicious.'

'Why do people put up with it?' Leonie asked.

Emilie shrugged. 'She is very beautiful and very rich, and with men she can be very good company, I believe.'

Leonie's eyes rested thoughtfully on Paul. Diane stood beside him, her hand on his arm in that possessive gesture, smiling at him. Paul had lost his frown, and was grinning, his eyes full of the amused indulgence a man might feel towards the playful aggression of a kitten.

Emilie looked, sighed. 'Yes, she is very dangerous. Believe me, you will have to be on your guard with her.'

'I doubt if I'll see much of her,' said Leonie. She

thought longingly of her uncomplicated life in London. How restful it would be to return to it, take up her daily routine and forget this Arabian Nights glamour which disguised a cold heart and a malicious mind.

If this was the world Paul inhabited she wanted no part of it. She would rather return to Comus and spend the next few months with Argon. He would be lonely there, and she was sure that he would welcome her return. Paul would not be able to complain, surely? It was only natural for her to stay with Argon when he was so ill?

Diane played the piano for them while they sat and listened with blank faces. Her touch was sure and delicate, yet the music, like the beautiful house, had no soul, and left one curiously unsatisfied. Diane was like a glittering mirror which reflects nothing but itself.

They left at eleven. As they walked to their car Emilie slipped close beside Leonie and whispered, 'Have dinner with us tomorrow—just you and Paul. I did not want to make the invitation publicly or I would have had to invite Diane.'

Leonie smiled warmly. 'I would love to, thank you.'

While Paul was unlocking the car Doris Nieman hurried up and made a similar invitation, adding shyly, 'Just you and Paul, no one else ... or would that be dull for you?'

'I would like it very much,' said Leonie, beginning to feel better.

Doris gave her a sweet smile. 'Good. I'll ring you

tomorrow. Perhaps we could do some shopping together? Carl always says it's my vice, but I just
adore Paris shops!'

In the car driving home, Paul said quietly, 'I am
sorry for Diane's behaviour.'

'I would prefer not to see much of her,' Leonie
said, deciding that there was no point in pretending
to like the woman. 'I'm sorry if that offends you...'

'No, I understand it, but George is a good friend
of mine, and Diane can be fun when she's not be-
having like a piranha. She's a man's woman. There's
no reason why you should see her apart from the
occasional dinner.' He shot her a look. 'You liked the
others, didn't you?'

'Yes, particularly Emilie. She's invited us to dinner tomorrow. Will that be convenient?'

'Yes, of course. I'm glad you're making friends
with little Emilie. She's a nice little thing.' He hesitated, then added, 'You have to realise that you're
coming into my world now. These are all old friends
of mine, business friends most of them, as well as
social ones. As my wife you will be expected to
become part of our circle.'

'Yes, I accept that,' she said. 'But Diane's behaviour is more than I can swallow.'

'It was outrageous,' he agreed. 'But that's Diane
... she won't change and we have to accept her.'

Leonie was silent.

After a while he said coolly, 'Jake, too. It would
be wisest for you to avoid him. He's a male version
of Diane.'

'I liked him,' she said deliberately, angry with his attitude to Diane.

'I noticed,' he said drily.

'Paul, I was thinking ... if Argon is really ill, shouldn't one of us be with him? I could fly back to Comus for a while. It would be obvious to everyone why I'd gone...'

'No,' Paul said decisively. 'You stay with me.'

'But Argon...'

'Argon would rather you stayed with me,' he said. 'All Argon wants is for you to get pregnant.'

Leonie felt a cruel twist of pain in her stomach and clenched her hands into two fists, biting her lip.

They arrived back at the flat in total silence. While Paul parked the car she went up to the flat and went into the bathroom. She showered and put on a nightdress, then went into the kitchen to make a nightcap. She heard Paul come in, walk along the hall. Doors clicked softly. Water ran. Leonie stirred the milky chocolate and hesitated for a moment, then tapped on the bathroom door.

'I've made some hot chocolate,' she said.

He emerged, towelling his hair. It was almost dark with water. His short towelling dressing-gown clung to his damp body, his bare legs making it plain he wore no pyjamas beneath it.

She turned away. 'I left your chocolate in the kitchen,' she said, moving towards her own bed-room.

Paul stood watching her as she closed the door. She put her drink down on her bedside table, flung her dressing-gown down on the bed and turned down the covers. She was about to get into bed when the door opened. She looked round, her heart in her throat. Paul stood there, staring at her.

His hand moved towards the light switch. Dry-mouthed, Leonie stood frozen to the spot as the room was plunged into darkness. Paul moved softly, quickly. A few seconds later she was in his arms, protesting, struggling.

His lips searched along her face as she twisted her head away. Her hair fell between them, and he nuzzled his way through the silky strands to find her mouth.

Against the hot invasion of his kiss she whispered frantically, 'No, Paul...'

Grimly, silently, he pushed her down on the bed and fell on top of her, his weight crushing her into breathless submission. Her brain was in angry panic. She loved him, but she did not want him to take her like this—she wanted his love, not his silent love-making. There was no tenderness in his kisses, only a fierce determination to compel her submission.

Then he raised himself above her. A pale glimmer of moonlight fell over her face. His features were partially visible, his eyes a quick glimmer as they searched her body in a comprehensive glance.

One hand was caressing her slowly, her naked shoulders, her breasts, her waist. She trembled under his touch. 'Don't, Paul,' she whispered faintly. 'Please, go away. I don't want you to...'

'You're my wife.'

'In name only,' she reminded him angrily. 'We made a bargain, and you must keep that bargain.'

'I can't,' he said, his voice harsh. 'I realised that tonight. Until you're mine I shall know no peace of mind. Jake suspects the truth—he said something to me tonight.'

'How could he guess——' She was incredulous.

Paul laughed fiercely. 'Jake is too experienced not to recognise innocence when he sees it. You don't have the look of a radiant young bride, my dear. You look ... untouched. And to a man like Jake that situation would be too tempting to resist.'

'Doesn't it occur to you that I can resist Jake?'

'Perhaps,' he said coolly. 'But what am I supposed to do while Jake is in hot pursuit? Ignore the situation? No—there's only one way out.' His voice was heavy, as though he was as reluctant as she was, and bitter pain welled up inside her. She pushed at his shoulders, wriggling to get away, but he was too strong for her. In a moment she was pinned to the bed again, his mouth descending in a kiss which drove all thought of anything but him out of her head.

Abandoning the struggle, she relaxed, and as if her body had only been waiting for her mind to relinquish control, a flood of sweet sensation washed over her.

Paul's hands moved sensually against her and she sobbed out his name, her own fingers searching against the hard muscled body above her, her desire beating up like a great flame.

Pleasure ached deep inside her, her limbs felt heavily languorous. Paul's lips parted against her throat, slid down slowly to her breasts. 'Darling,' he murmured. 'I won't hurt you.'

Leonie barely heard him. Through a mist of pleasure and desire she heard herself saying his name over and over again, her voice weak with total surrender.

CHAPTER SEVEN

LIGHT was dancing under her eyelids. She reluctantly opened them and found the room flooded with
sunlight and Paul moving beween the bed and the
window, his body fully clothed in a dark suit.

For a few seconds she only stared at him, still
drugged with the deepest, sweetest sleep of her life.
Then memory washed back into her mind and she
shrank back against the pillows, her cheeks growing
scarlet.

Paul walked to the door. 'I brought you your
breakfast,' he said coolly. 'Tea and toast. I hope it's
what you wanted. I'm afraid I have to go out—I
have a business meeting at ten-thirty. I'll be back by
one o'clock and we'll go out to lunch.'

'Can't I cook something here?' she asked shyly.

'I would rather go out,' he said curtly, as he closed
the door and vanished.

Leonie lay listening to the sound of his footsteps,
then the bang of the front door. Last night might
have been a dream. They were back in reality, in the
cold steel trap of their marriage, two strangers living
together in a pretence which grew more difficult to
sustain with every passing day.

She closed her eyes, groaning. How could she
have been so lost to self-respect that she had let him
make love to her, that she had met him half way, in

the end, and responded passionately to his love-making? She despised herself. She had been weak.

She pulled herself together, sat up and leant over to get her tea. As she did so her eye caught sight of the glint of gold on the pillow, a fine short hair which she recognised as one of Paul's. The sight of it sent a hot wave sweeping over her body as she remembered other moments during the night, the naked brush of his body against her as she slid into sleep, the tingle of his mouth on her throat, her own voice sobbing in surrender.

When she had nibbled at her toast and drunk her tea, she got out of bed. The mirror gave her back her own reflection, her slim nakedness glowing white in the sun-filled room. She saw faint bruises on her flesh, the marks of love, and hurriedly turned away to find some clothes.

Later, showered and dressed, she went out to find a grey-haired woman vacuum-cleaning the carpets while a radio blared out pop music in the background. The woman turned to smile at her.

'*Bonjour, madame. Je suis* Madame Delarge.'

'Good morning,' Leonie said uncertainly. This must be the woman who cleaned the flat. She had not come yesterday, but Paul had mentioned her.

They exchanged a few polite words, then the telephone rang, and Leonie went to answer it. It was Doris Nieman, her voice friendly and eager.

'Will you come shopping this morning?'

'I would like to,' Leonie said, pleased to have someone to talk to this morning. Anything which would take her mind off the previous night was welcome.

She scribbled a hasty note for Paul, in case he should return early, and went down to meet Doris when her car drew up.

'Is there something you particularly want to buy?' she asked as the car moved back into the traffic.

Doris laughed. 'My dear, I want to buy thousands of things—I always do. But today I'm just browsing, and that's the way I like it best. I'm an impulse buyer. I browse and snatch at interesting little titbits. It drives Carl mad.'

'It sounds fun,' Leonie smiled. She had never been able to afford such haphazard shopping, when she bought something it was because she needed it, she planned ahead and organised her shopping, whether of food or clothes. Living on a limited income made one cost-conscious.

They parked and wandered along the wide, elegant shopping centres, sauntering beside plate glass windows and gazing at the objects displayed with the contented appraisal of people who are just amusing themselves. Doris halted to make a detailed inspection of a pale calf handbag.

'Nice, don't you think?'

There was no price ticket, but Leonie suspected that she would find the price shocking. But she said, 'Very nice, indeed.'

Doris chewed on her lower lip. 'I think ... yes, I really think I might ... but first I must find shoes to match ... we can come back when we've found them ...'

They found the shoes half a mile away. By then Leonie's legs and feet were throbbing with exhaustion. Doris, however, seemed untiring. When she had tried the shoes, bought them and left the shop, she looked at Leonie with a twinkle in her eyes.

'My dear girl, you look half dead!' She turned and snapped her fingers with the easy expectation of the rich and at once a taxi materialised out of thin air. Leonie was admiringly awe-struck. She had always found it impossible to find a taxi when she wanted one.

They arrived at the shop in which they had seen the handbag, bought it and left again. Then Doris drove Leonie back to Paul's flat, talking cheerfully about her husband, her friends and life in general.

'A pity you had to meet Diane on your first evening,' she said. 'But Paul may have been wise. Sometimes it's best to take the worst fence first. The others seem easy afterwards.'

Leonie laughed. 'So you don't like her, either?'

'Who does?' said Doris.

'George?'

'That poor squashed worm,' said Doris.

Leonie could not help smiling, but she said, 'I liked George, actually.'

'Everyone does, but remember, honey, George chose to marry Diane of his own free will. That makes him a fool in my book. Even a blind man could see what sort of poisonous female she was ...'

'We can't always choose where we love,' Leonie said. 'She's very beautiful.'

'So is a viper, but they're both deadly.'

Doris dropped her at the flat and drove off, waving. Leonie found Paul already back, his hands restlessly fingering the edges of the book he was reading.

He looked up as she entered the room and laid down his book. 'There you are! I was beginning to wonder what had happened to you.' The blue eyes searched hers intently. 'You say you were with Doris?'

'We went shopping.' Leonie sank into a chair and slipped off her shoes, bending to massage her ankles wearily. 'When Doris goes shopping she really takes it seriously. I'm exhausted!'

Paul crouched down and took one of her ankles in his hand, rubbing finger and thumb gently over the fine bones, while he looked up at her.

'See anybody else?'

His tone struck her as odd. She frowned. 'No. Why?'

'I just wondered,' he said.

She stared at him. 'Wondered what?'

'Jake rang before I left,' he said curtly. 'He asked if we would have lunch with him, but I refused.'

She flushed. 'So you suspected me of secretly meeting him this morning? Thanks! You certainly trust me, don't you?'

'I trust you. I don't trust Jake.'

'Paul, I'm not in the habit of lying. If I see Jake I'll tell you. I won't make a big secret of it.'

He nodded, looking down at her feet. 'You have lovely feet, did you know? Long and slender, beautifully formed.'

Her heart began to pound in her breast. She was shaken by his tone.

'Your legs are lovely, too,' he went on, in the same voice. His hand moved slowly up her calf, the fingers caressing. 'You're a very desirable woman. I don't blame Jake for wanting you. I saw right from the start that he was very attracted. I should have realised he would be, but I didn't expect him to arrive on the scene so soon.' He lifted his blue gaze to her face. 'Jake is a very experienced hunter. Don't underestimate him. He'll use any weapon, however unscrupulous, to get his own way.'

'All right, you've warned me. Now can we go and get some lunch? I'm starving.'

He stood up. Leonie slipped back into her shoes, wincing as she stood up. Paul grinned.

'Poor girl, you do look tired.'

'Next time I go shopping with Doris I'll take a wheelchair!'

He laughed. 'Carl often complains about her shopping. He refuses to go with her, but she likes to have company on her treks around town.'

'Thanks for the warning.'

They went out to lunch at a large restaurant near the Seine. The bay windows looked out over the river. The blue sky shimmered in a heat haze and seagulls skimmed low over the water, screaming for fish.

Paul ordered the meal, saying that Leonie could trust him not to order anything she did not like. 'I think I know your tastes by now.'

He had ordered fresh sardines followed by roast

beef French style, the meat pink and moist in thick rectangular slices, served with salad and sauté potatoes.

Leonie was so hungry that she would have eaten almost anything, but the superb cooking impressed her considerably.

After lunch they drove into the French countryside for a few hours, lingering at will wherever they saw something interesting. It was an enchanting interlude stolen from the over-sophisticated city life of the night before, like wandering into a fairy tale for a few hours, and Leonie wished it need never end. Paul was a gay, charming companion, gentle and sympathetic, filled with deep enthusiasm for France and its landscapes, telling her old French legends and fairy tales, talking warmly about French food and French wine.

'You really love this country,' she said, watching his handsome face as he fell silent.

'Very much,' he agreed, turning his head to smile. A lock of blond hair fell over his forehead in a smooth swathe, and she felt a sudden longing to reach up with her hand and push it back just to feel the silkiness of it under her fingers.

Their eyes met, and Paul's blue gaze suddenly darkened. He reached out for her with one long-fingered hand. Helpless to resist, she let him pull her close, turned her mouth up towards him and was engulfed by a rush of blind passion which shook her to her soul. The warm sunshine, the peaceful afternoon, had lulled her into drowsy content, weakening her power of resistance. She clung to him, pulses clamouring, and knew fatally that if he came to her again tonight she would never be able to send him away.

When he drew back his mouth she made a low moan of protest, her lids tightly closed, her hands still clinging to him. Paul started the engine again and she reluctantly opened her eyes, releasing him. He drove in silence, his brows drawn together in a dark line. She wondered why he looked so angry. Was he furious with himself for making love to her again? His reactions were inexplicable. She had ceased to believe she would ever make sense of him. When they made their original bargain it had been clear between them that their marriage would be one of convenience, yet Paul had now insisted on making her his wife in passionate reality. Apparently his decision had been dictated by a desire to make sure she did not enter into a flirtation with Jake Tennyson and cause some sort of scandal. Yet he had made love to her so hotly; her body had recognised the feel of real passion, even though her mind had doubted him. What did he really feel towards her? Did he still resent their marriage? Had his passionate lovemaking been in some way a punishment, a revenge?

It was difficult to reconcile the curt, angry man who had been her usual companion since they arrived in Paris with the man who had just made love to her, or with the charming, teasing stranger she had known on Comus.

That evening they had dinner with Emilie and Klaus, who lived in a discreetly expensive flat several streets away from them. Emilie was a cheerful, casual hostess, chattering to Leonie in the corner of a huge white sofa while Paul and Klaus leaned against a bookcase and talked soberly of business.

'Look at them,' Emilie said under her breath. 'Like little boys talking about football. Men never grow up, do they? They play their games all their lives.'

'Don't women, too? As little girls we play at being mothers, with our dolls. I suppose all children's games are practising for adult life.'

'Ah, but with us it is real when we grow up. With men—never. Work is still a game to them. They have to win, whether it is a business deal or a woman. It is all a question of status. But with women, the business of having children makes us suddenly adult. Then we have charge of another life and that is a sobering situation.' Emilie laughed. 'One I shall have to face soon.'

'You're expecting a baby?' Leonie was thrilled. 'When?'

'Oh, six months to go yet. We are not telling people for the moment. Once everyone knows I shall start being left out of parties. I've seen it before—a pregnant woman is treated like an imbecile ... oh, poor girl, they say. She won't want to come in her condition!' Emilie grimaced. 'So don't tell anyone, will you?'

'Of course not. Is Klaus pleased?'

'Pleased? He is ecstatic. Anyone would think he managed it all by himself.' Emilie grinned. 'He would like to go around boasting to the whole

world. I have had trouble persuading him to keep it
to himself. I think Diane suspects, though. Did you
notice her little dig at me last night? Diane is a cat,
but she has intuition, and of course, she is particularly quick to sense when anyone else is pregnant.'

Leonie looked a question.

Emilie leaned closer and lowered her voice.
'Diane cannot have babies. She and George wanted
them, but the doctors have said it is impossible, and
it is Diane who can't have them, not George.'

'I wonder if that's why ... poor Diane!'

'Of course, it explains a great deal,' nodded
Emilie. 'But I'm afraid it does not make me like her
any better. She is so spiteful.'

'She must be very bitter,' said Leonie, thinking of
Diane's curved, pink and gold ripeness. Who would
have suspected by looking at her that she was unable
to have children? If any woman looked built for
motherhood it was Diane. She looked the very
essence of fertility.

'It is George I am most sorry for—he would make
a wonderful father.'

'Who would?' Klaus asked, approaching on the
last words. His face looked blandly teasing as he
eyed his young wife.

'Not you, anyway,' said Emilie with a grin.

'Paul?' Klaus turned to give Paul a broad smile.
'Don't tell me you are already expecting a happy
event?' His brows rose in amused enquiry.

Paul flushed darkly. 'No,' he said tightly. 'Not to
my knowledge.' His blue eyes flashed an angry
question at Leonie.

'We were talking about a third party,' said Emilie. 'But I have told Leonie our secret, darling.'

Klaus beamed. 'Well, I'm glad to have one excuse for breaking out the cigars and best brandy,' he said delightedly.

'What's this?' Paul looked at Emilie with a smile. 'Do I gather that it's Klaus after all who will make a wonderful father?'

'I hope so,' Emilie said, laughing. 'He had better! Or I will know the reason why.'

'No brandy for you then,' said Paul, nodding.

'You see?' Emilie sighed, turning to give Leonie a comical look of disgust. 'It starts at once. If Klaus had his way I would be rolled in cotton wool for the next six months and put in a cupboard.'

'No, darling,' Klaus corrected her. 'In a lovely glass case where I could look at you every day! Like Snow White.'

'It was the seven ugly little dwarfs who put her in the case,' Emilie pointed out. 'She had to wait for the Prince to let her out.'

'In our case it is reversed,' said Klaus. 'The Prince will put you in and an ugly little dwarf will arrive to let you out.'

'Are you calling my baby an ugly little dwarf?' She was indignant.

'Most babies are,' said Klaus, his teasing barely concealing his joy.

'Not mine,' she said with determination. 'My baby will be exquisite and brilliant.'

'Like me,' Klaus nodded.

She punched him lightly. 'What vanity!'

They all laughed and the evening flowed on in the same happy vein. Emilie's news seemed to give them all a feeling of warm pleasure which cast a glow over the evening.

When they were back in their own flat the sensation remained with them. Paul hummed softly as he made hot chocolate for them both. Leonie turned on the radio and found some soft dance music on a late-night show.

Paul turned and looked at her, his blue eyes veiled by their half-lowered lids.

'Do you ever think of that fellow in England?' he asked her abruptly.

Leonie looked blank. 'What fellow in England?' Then she realised what he meant, and felt herself flush. 'No,' she said quickly.

'You must have been badly in love with him to be so hurt,' Paul said.

'I was naïve enough to be taken in by a good line of patter,' she shrugged.

'I remember you once told me I reminded you of him,' Paul said softly, watching her. 'Does that still apply?'

She flushed. 'No. I'm sorry I said it. It wasn't true, of course. I was just...'

'Sticking the knife in?'

'I suppose so,' she admitted unhappily.

'And you have no secret hankering for him?' Paul asked.

'None at all,' she said firmly.

He moved towards her slowly, his eyes holding

hers. Just then the telephone rang. Paul cursed under his breath.

'Who on earth can that be at this hour?' He moved quickly into the next room. The ringing stopped. Leonie heard his voice, curt and peremptory. 'Yes?' Then silence. Then a low exclamation of shocked dismay.

'My God! But how...' Silence followed. Then Paul said gently, 'Yes, of course, Diane. I'll be there right away.'

Diane? Leonie felt a sharp stab of jealousy. Why was Diane ringing Paul at this time of night? And why was Paul prepared to go out obediently at her lightest request? What had there been between them before Paul flew to Comus? Could the relationship have been deeper than everyone supposed? Was it true, as Emilie had told her, that Paul was just one of Diane's circle of admiring males? Or was there something more serious between the two of them? Diane's malice towards her had been so personal that Leonie's feminine intuition told her Diane had suffered from bitter jealousy towards her.

Paul appeared in the doorway, shrugging into his jacket again, his shirt open at the neck, exposing the strong brown column of his throat.

She looked at him calmly, masking her fear.

'I have to go out,' he said. 'That was Diane. George has had a heart attack.'

'Oh, no!' She was aghast at her own earlier thoughts. 'Poor George!' Then, from shame at herself, 'Poor Diane! Is there anything I can do? Would you like me to come with you?'

Shaking his head Paul said, 'No, get off to bed. You look tired. They've taken George to hospital. Diane wanted someone to talk to while she waits for news. She's in a state of shock, which isn't surprising. George has always looked so healthy. This is a very unexpected development. Coming so suddenly it's knocked her completely off balance. I've never heard Diane sound so distraught.'

'She must be very worried,' nodded Leonie.

Paul sighed. 'Yes, of course. Well, goodnight. Don't stay up late. You need some sleep.'

When he had gone Leonie slowly tidied up, put out all the lights, showered and slipped into her nightdress, then got into bed. She could not relax; her mind was far too active. She tossed and turned on her pillows, consumed with anxiety.

She remembered Diane's cold contempt towards her husband at that dinner party. Could that have masked real affection? Somehow Leonie did not believe it. Diane did not love George. No doubt his heart attack had been a shock to her, but Leonie found it disturbing that it should have been to Paul that Diane turned at such a moment.

If George died Diane would be free...

She sat up restlessly, biting her lip. Such a thought was cruel in the circumstances, selfish and petty, yet it would not be banished.

If Diane was free what effect would that have on Paul, on their marriage? How did Paul really feel towards Diane?

Thinking of the other woman's blonde beauty Leonie could only feel miserably afraid. She had no weapons to combat Diane's sophisticated loveliness. Diane had the advantage of having known Paul for years, of sharing a past with him.

Her head began to ache intolerably. She padded into the bathroom and found some aspirin in the cupboard. Taking two with a glass of water, she settled down in bed again with a book, a detective story she had found in Paul's bookcase.

Somehow she managed to concentrate on the involved plot, but the characters were so bizarre and the background so gothic that she could not engage herself with the story. At last her eyelids began to droop. She put out the light and fell slowly to sleep.

When she woke up she heard the vacuum cleaner humming in another room. Daylight lay over the room like a pall. She slid out of bed and moved to the window. It was a grey morning with a smell of rain in the air. It matched her mood.

Madame Delarge was cheerful as she passed, bidding her a brisk good-morning.

Leonie felt numb and depressed. She drank some chilled orange juice, sipped at a cup of strong coffee, looked through the Paris newspapers, practising her schoolgirl French. She had made up her mind to read a newspaper once a day in order to improve her grasp of the language, but today the print blurred before her eyes.

Paul was not back yet. His room stood empty, the bed still neat and unused.

Doris rang at eleven. 'Have you heard?'

'About George? Yes.'

'Do you know the latest bulletin?'

'I only know he had a heart attack last night and is in hospital,' Leonie said.

'Paul rang Carl this morning. Apparently George is holding his own, but only just. It's touch and go.'

'How is Diane taking it?' Leonie had to ask. Paul had not rung her. He had rung his friends, but he had not rung her. What did that indicate? What was going on between those two at the hospital?

Doris made a little grunt of disgust. 'Who knows? Paul said she was very distressed, but you know Diane! She has one face for men, another for women. I'd like to see for myself before I believed anything about her.'

'It must have been a shock to her!'

'Oh, at first, no doubt. But she has such a cold mind. Who knows what thoughts occurred to her after the first shock passed?'

'We mustn't be uncharitable,' Leonie protested. 'One never knows the truth about what happens between two people, particularly husband and wife.'

'True,' Doris agreed. She laughed gently. 'You're very sweet, you know that? Has Paul been there with all her night?'

The question was charged with danger. Leonie controlled her voice carefully. 'Yes. We thought he should stay with her.'

Doris was silent for a moment, then she said, 'Chin up, honey. How about lunch with me today? Carl has a business lunch.'

'Thank you, but I think I'd better stay here in case Paul needs me.'

'You know best, honey,' Doris said quietly.

When she had rung off, Leonie moved into the kitchen and looked at the food available. Salad would be a simple meal, easily prepared, if Paul came back.

If Paul came back...

Madame Delarge finished her work and departed, and Leonie sat in the kitchen drinking coffee and waiting. The hours dragged past. At one o'clock she reluctantly prepared a very small plate of salad and ate it without enthusiasm.

Why had Paul not rung her? He must know she would be worried. Was Diane so possessive, so clinging, that he could not leave her even for a moment or two?

Or had he merely forgotten her own existence?

At three o'clock someone rang the doorbell, giving her a shock that made her leap up out of her chair, quivering.

She almost ran to the door. Had Paul forgotten his key? But when she opened the door it was to find Jake leaning against the doorframe, casually dressed in a denim suit with a very elegant navy blue silk shirt showing beneath it.

She stared at him blankly. 'Oh, it's you.' Disappointment made her voice stark.

He lifted one thin eyebrow. 'I'm sorry. Who did you think it was?' He glanced past her. 'Paul not here?'

'Haven't you heard? George has had a heart attack. Paul is at the hospital.'

Jake's eyes narrowed acutely. 'Comforting the

lovely Diane? Of course. He would be.'

Leonie felt icy cold. 'Is there any message?' she asked.

Jake put out a hand and lifted her chin, his fingers cool. 'You look like a ghost—do you know that? What you need is a drink. I've got my car outside. Come on...'

She hung back. 'No. I must wait here in case Paul comes back and needs me.'

Jake's lip curled. 'Don't be a doormat, darling. It never pays in the end.'

The tone pricked her pride. She hesitated, then shrugged. 'Oh, very well. But I must leave him a note.'

Jake followed her back into the flat, watched as she left a note for Paul and waited while she changed into a different dress and renewed her make-up.

They drove to a small wine bar in a quiet quarter of the city, and sat drinking Provençal wine and eating tiny snippets of various cheeses with fresh, buttery croissant, in a corner of the half empty room.

Jake talked about Provence, enthused about the *langue d'oc*, the ancient tongue of the region, long since fallen into disuse, but enshrining some very lovely poetry which was still much admired today. 'I've a house there,' he said. 'Well, a cottage, really, a peasant's cottage with a rose-pink roof and no sanitation to speak of—one day I'll take you there. You'll love it.' His eyes skimmed her face. 'There aren't many people I would invite to the place. I love it too much to have intruders there. But you would get the feel of the atmosphere, I'm sure of that.'

'You know nothing about me,' Leonie protested. 'We've only met twice, very briefly.'

'With some people once is enough,' Jake said simply.

She looked at him in sharp question. His eyes were direct and honest at this moment, but she felt a prickle of warning. Was Paul right? Was Jake attracted to her? And how far could she trust this very attractive, very experienced man of the world? Her experience of men was not varied enough to make her sure of herself, and her one real love affair had ended so badly that she did not trust her judgment of men.

Jake saw the doubt in her face and smiled wryly. 'Paul has warned you against my wicked wiles, I gather.'

'He told me you were something of a Don Juan,' she admitted, smiling.

'My dear, I'm not in Paul's league,' he commented drily.

She bit her lip. 'I would rather not discuss my husband,' she told him.

Jake grinned. 'Fair enough. Tell me about yourself instead. Where were you born, what have you done with yourself all your life?'

'I was born in England,' she said. 'You know that. I went to school there, I went on to art college and I got a job as a commercial artist...' She talked about her work and Jake listened. He was a good listener. He asked the right questions, seemed very interested. She found herself telling him about her disastrous love affair, and wondered how it had come about. He had a way of winkling facts out of one without one knowing what was going on.

'You're really very green, aren't you?' he asked her with gentle amusement.

She flushed but laughed. 'I suppose so.'

He put out a finger to stroke her cheek. 'It's a delightful innocence, though, as Paul has no doubt told you. The combination is quite irresistible.'

She drew away from his caress, frowning. 'Combination? What combination?'

He stared at her almost hypnotically. 'Why, that innocence combined with the promise of passion in your face ... you have a very sensual mouth, a full lower lip with a deliciously curved upper lip, and your eyes are like those of a wild, shy bird.'

She laughed. 'Good lord! Is this your famous technique for seduction? I'm afraid it wouldn't work with me. It makes me want to giggle.'

Something gleamed in his eyes, an answering amusement. 'Does it, indeed? I obviously need a different approach.'

'Don't bother. I'm not interested.' She met his glance squarely. 'I mean that. I don't want to offend you, Jake, but I don't intend to get involved with you.'

He ran his eyes over her slowly. 'Now that's a pity, because I find you very attractive.'

She flushed. 'Thank you, but still...'

'Still no?' He grinned. Well, that clears the air,

doesn't it? Tell me, is it Paul?'

Her eyes dropped away, her colour deepening.

'I see it is,' he said softly. 'Well, well, well! Lucky Paul. I'll drive you back to the flat, shall I?'

'Thank you.'

As they drove, he asked her curiously, 'Shall you tell him you've been out with me? What did you say in your note?'

'Just that I was going out for a drink,' she admitted. Her chin lifted defiantly. 'But I shall tell him it was with you.'

'He won't like it.'

'No,' she agreed. 'But then...' She bit the words off quickly, but not quickly enough.

'But then...' Jake glanced at her shrewdly. 'But then you don't like him being with Diane?' he guessed.

She grimaced. 'Obvious, aren't I?'

'No, I think you're very wise,' Jake said. 'Jealousy can have a salutary effect.'

'Jealousy is poison,' she said deeply.

He glanced at her again. 'Poor girl! That bad? Tell me, was I right in supposing your marriage to be an arranged match?'

She hesitated. 'What made you think that?'

Jake grinned. 'Paul hadn't even met you before he went to Comus. Yet he married you almost at once, and since you're his cousin I suspect the idea emanated from old Argon. Keep the money in the family —shrewd business sense.'

'Is that what everyone thinks?'

'I imagine so. Paul has been a bachelor gay for

years. He was generally reckoned to be marriage-proof. His rapid marriage to the only other heir to all that money could have only one explanation.' Jake studied her curiously. 'Were you in love with him before you married him? Or did that happen afterwards?'

Leonie gave him a slight smile. 'Do you really expect me to answer that?'

Jake laughed. 'Perhaps not. There's only one other question I would like to know the answer to ... do you and Paul sleep together?'

Hot colour flooded her face. 'Honestly, you have the cheek of the devil!'

Jake watched her face intently. 'My guess is ... no.'

Her lids fluttered, and a slight smile touched her mouth.

Jake drew in his breath sharply. 'On the other hand, maybe I'm wrong...' She looked up in surprise, and he met her eyes soberly. 'Paul takes no chances, does he? Under that playboy exterior the Caprel blood tells. He bolted the stable door before the horse could escape.'

'You really shouldn't say such things to me,' she protested quickly, her cheeks flaming.

'I'm only talking to myself,' he said lightly. 'I wonder if I'm right, though. When we first met at the flat Paul's violent reaction towards me left me slightly puzzled. After I'd thought about it for a while, though, it occurred to me that if the marriage was, as we all suspected, an arranged one, Paul might well feel nervous about any other man taking an interest in you. If you were not sleeping together there would be no problem if one of you wanted to dissolve the marriage. Naturally, in those circumstances, Paul was on edge, so he lost no time in altering the situation. In his place I'd have done the same.'

'You make it sound very cold-blooded,' she said faintly, her lips trembling. Wasn't that exactly what it had been? A cold-blooded decision by Paul to ensure her own fidelity?

Jake drew up outside the flat, switched off the engine and turned to look gently at her. 'Only you know the truth. I was merely speculating. I'm flying back to England today. If ever you need a disinterested friend get in touch.' He met her eyes quietly. 'I mean just that—a friend. No strings, no consequences.'

She was touched. 'Thank you.'

'You have an integrity I find very attractive,' he said in an offhanded way. 'A word of advice? If you want Paul, forget the rules. Play to win.'

Leonie laughed. 'I'll have to see. I'm not sure I would want to win that way.'

Jake's face tightened. He took one of her hands, lifted it to his lips and kissed the back with bent head for a moment.

Pulling her hand away, Leonie hurriedly got out of the car and almost ran into the building, her pulses beating fast. Just for that second, something inside herself had reacted instinctively towards Jake, and she was alarmed. She began to see why Paul had been afraid when Jake showed an interest in her. Jake was dangerous.

She found her key, fitted it into the lock and was turning it when the door was flung open and she found herself confronting Paul; Paul in a mood she did not recognise, with tightened lips and blazing eyes. The air crackled with menace as they faced each other.

CHAPTER EIGHT

'I was watching from the window,' he said between tight teeth. 'Very touching, the way Jake kissed your hand. He wasn't here all night, I suppose?'

'What a foul accusation!' She stiffened with rage. 'I'm not one of your promiscuous, bed-hopping lady-friends!'

He pulled her through the door, slammed it behind them and leaned over her, his tall figure looming threateningly, his glittering eyes pinning her like a butterfly to the wall.

'I seem to remember I had no trouble getting you into bed,' he snarled.

Her hand shot up, slapped him hard across his smiling face. The sound seemed to echo between them endlessly.

Paul put up a hand slowly to his cheek. 'You little vixen!'

'You deserved it,' she said huskily.

After a moment of silence, while their eyes warred, he asked, 'How long have you been with Jake?'

'A few hours. He asked me out for a drink. I was bored and lonely. You hadn't rung, I had no idea where you were, or what you were doing.' Her eyes lifted, accusing him silently. 'I only knew you were with Diane all night.'

'Whose husband is dangerously ill,' he pointed out icily.

'Whose husband may die leaving her free to marry again,' she shot back angrily.

'My God, women can be cold-blooded at times!' he said bitterly.

'We aren't the only ones!' Leonie thought of him making love to her simply to make sure she did not encourage Jake. How dare he call her cold-blooded!

'I told you never to go out with Jake,' he snapped.

'You don't own me! I'm free to do as I please. What did you expect? That I should sit here like a Victorian wife waiting for my lord and master to deign to come home? Why didn't you ring me?'

'I meant to,' he said, restlessly. 'I just never had the time. Diane was in such a state, I hardly dared to leave her for a moment.'

'You managed to ring Carl and give him the news!'

He flushed. 'Yes. Diane asked me to ring Carl because George had an appointment with him today and Carl had to be told why George wouldn't keep it.'

'But she wouldn't let you ring me, of course,' Leonie said flatly.

Their eyes met. Paul flushed. 'She was distraught. I couldn't do anything which would upset her any more...'

'I didn't matter, anyway, did I? Only Diane mattered.'

He caught her shoulders. 'It wasn't like that.'

'What was it like? Tell me. I'm sure you can think up a very plausible excuse if you try.'

'Oh, for God's sake,' he said, turning away. 'George is so ill, I had to humour her.'

'How did you manage to get away now? I'm surprised she let you go.'

'Her sister arrived from Nice and took charge. She made Diane take a sleeping pill and go to bed.'

'I'm sure you could have managed to get Diane to bed without the aid of sleeping pills,' she flung.

'Don't talk like that!'

'You accused me of spending the night with Jake on far more slender evidence,' she reminded him.

He looked at her, frowning. 'I'm sorry, I shouldn't have said that. I know it was a ridiculous suggestion...'

'Oh, I don't know,' she retorted. 'As you said, Jake is very attractive.'

Paul came softly towards her, menace in every line. He took her chin in his hand and lifted her face towards him, his blue eyes as bright and cold as sapphires. 'Don't torment me, Leonie. I'm not the man to stand for it.'

She remembered Jake's advice to play to win. Excitement made her whole body shiver. Softly, she said, 'Do I torment you, Paul?'

'Leonie...' Her name was sighed out so faintly she barely heard it. He released her and turned away. Standing with his back to her, he said, 'It must wait.'

She watched him. 'What must?'

He shrugged. 'I have to get back to the hospital in an hour. George has recovered consciousness and is asking for his solicitor. He was in the process of changing his will, it seems, and he wants to sign the new one. He has named me one of the executors and he wants me present when he signs.'

'Oh.' She sighed. 'George isn't going to die, is he?'

'I hope not. He's lived through the first twenty-four hours after the attack and that's a good sign, apparently. With care he should pull through, but he'll never be able to run his business as he used to—he'll have to take it easy in future. God knows how he'll take that news. He's never been able to delegate. He's always overworked. I don't know if George knows how to rest.'

'Poor George!'

'Yes, poor George,' Paul agreed. 'I think I'll take a shower and then have a meal. Is there anything to eat?'

'I'll fix you something. What would you like? I could make an omelette.'

'That sounds perfect,' he said gratefully, moving towards the bathroom.

Leonie went into the kitchen and began to prepare the eggs. She found some cheese and some tomatoes, buttered some croissants and made a pot of coffee.

When Paul reappeared ten minutes later, immaculately dressed in a dark suit and blue shirt, the table was laid. 'Sit down,' she urged, and quickly placed the cheese and tomato omelette before him. While she poured him coffee, he began to eat.

'This is delicious,' he said. 'You're a good cook.'

She set his cup on the table. 'If you're still hungry, there's plenty of fruit.'

'Any grapes?' he asked, sipping the coffee.

She lifted a stalk of purple grapes on to a plate and offered it to him. Paul leaned back in his chair, popping the fruit into his mouth in a leisurely fashion. 'What about you?' he asked. 'Or did Jake feed you?'

'We had a drink, that's all,' she said quickly. 'I'll eat later.'

Paul shot her a narrow-eyed look. 'With Jake?'

'Of course not!'

'You forget, I saw him kiss your hand just now. Once Jake is on the trail he never gives up. He'll be back.'

'He flies to England today,' she said.

Paul stared at her. 'Did he say that?'

'Yes.'

'Hmm ... I wonder.'

'I'm sure he meant it,' she said.

Paul relaxed. 'Well, he couldn't afford to spend much more time here. Business is pretty brisk over there.' He gave her another sharp look. 'Sorry he's going?'

'I barely know the man.'

Paul's mouth twisted. 'Tell me the truth, Leonie. You do find him attractive, don't you? I knew that right from the first day—I saw it between the two of you when I came into the kitchen. Sexual attraction shows, you know.'

She flushed. 'Jake is attractive, yes.' Then she added quickly, 'But so are a lot of other men. It takes a lot more than that to make anything happen between two people. Physical attraction is only part of the story.'

'How fascinating,' he drawled mockingly. 'Do tell me more. What other ingredients are necessary?'

'Don't make fun of me—I'm serious. Respect is necessary, so is friendship. I would need to like and respect any man I fell in love with.'

'And did you like and respect the chap in England?' he asked sardonically.

'That was what taught me the need for both,' she returned. 'I was blinded by physical attraction that time. In future I shall want to know much more about any man.'

'What do you know about me?' he asked, staring at her.

She flushed. 'I know you're spoilt and self-centred,' she flung at him.

Paul grimaced. 'And that puts me out of the running, does it? Prince Charming would never be either.'

She did not reply. There was nothing she could say without betraying herself.

Insistently, he asked her, 'Well, Leonie?'

She stared at the floor. 'You altered everything between us when you insisted on making love to me.'

There was silence. 'You'll never forgive me for that, will you?' Paul asked thickly. 'I knew it next morning. You wouldn't even look at me. I've bitterly regretted it ever since. I lost my head, but that's no excuse. I can only apologise.' He stood up, his chair falling with a crash. 'I think you'd better do as you suggested, fly to Comus and stay with Argon. You and I would be better apart for the moment.'

Leonie stared at him, her breath hurting in her lungs. He was sending her away from him, packing her back to Comus like an unwanted kitten. Diane took precedence now. Diane, soon to be free to marry. Would Paul write in a few months and suggest a quiet divorce? No wonder he now regretted that night of love. Had he not been so precipitate he might have been able to have the marriage annulled without trouble, but now they could not claim that they had never consummated their marriage.

Had it been for Diane's sake that Paul had never married before? All those girls, those beautiful actresses and models with whom he had been seen around, had they been a cover for his real love? Had they been a smoke-screen designed to disguise from George what was going on between Paul and his wife?

Paul moved quickly out of the room, and Leonie listened as the front door slammed.

He had gone. The sound seemed to echo in the flat, and inside her head. She closed her eyes as tears forced their way between her lids and trickled down her cheeks.

After a moment she got up and began to clear the kitchen, wash up the utensils she had used and restore the room to order. That done, she went through to the sitting-room and lifted the telephone.

Later, she packed her clothes in a suitcase, took a last look around the flat and put her front door key down on the kitchen table. There was no need to leave a note. Paul would know where she had gone.

In the taxi she fought a bitter struggle with her love, but her pride won. Paul had told her to go. She would do just that. Their marriage had been a bitter experience, and she had had enough of pain, humiliation and misery.

She spent that night in a noisy little hotel in Athens. A taverna across the street throbbed with the beat of a bouzouki. Cars hooted and raced their engines up and down the road. Somewhere a dog was howling. Leonie could not sleep; it was too hot. She sat by the window, peering through the slats of the blind at the bright lights of the city.

Along the coast road she could see the lights of cars moving like fireflies. Aircraft flew low over the Aegean as they came to land at the airport. Planes seemed to arrive every few moments.

Dawn came slowly, bringing a temporary coolness. She washed, dressed, stared at herself disparagingly in the mirror. She was pale and stiff-lipped. Argon would know as soon as he set eyes on her that something was wrong. She forced a smile and the pale lips moved quiveringly apart. Somehow she had to keep up a pretence of being perfectly happy.

She barely noticed the rest of the journey; the flight to Comus passed like a dream, the drive from the landing strip to the villa followed in the same vague haze.

Only when she met Clyte at the terrace door did anything penetrate the cloak in which she had wrapped herself, and she gave the old woman a bright, stiff smile.

Clyte looked at her with concern. 'You look ill! What is wrong? Why are you here alone? We tried to ring Paul, but there was no reply at the flat.'

'I'm just tired, not ill. Don't worry. Paul's best friend has collapsed with a heart attack and he's very busy taking care of things for him. We thought I would be better off here with Argon for the moment. Paul is too busy to spend much time with me and I hardly know a soul in Paris.'

Clyte's dark eyes searched hers. 'Is that true?'

Leonie smiled again, that stiff unreal smile. 'Of course. It was my idea at first—I was worried about Argon. Paul agreed after he had realised how little free time he would have at present.'

'Come up to Argon,' Clyte said seriously, still not convinced. 'Tell him.'

Leonie followed her up the stairs, feeling nervous. Would Argon press questions on her? She was terrified of breaking down in front of him. She must not let him guess how bad things were between her and Paul.

Argon was waiting for her, sitting up against his piled pillows with a frown creasing his forehead. Leonie ran to him and bent to kiss his cheek. He put up a hand to touch her hair gently, and over her bent head his eyes met Clyte's. The two old people exchanged looks of mutual understanding, then Clyte softly left the room.

'So,' Argon said, pushing Leonie slightly away so that he could see her face. 'You have come back to Comus.'

'Yes,' she said hastily, and told him about George's heart attack and the need for Paul to take charge of affairs while George was out of action.

'This man is not one of the family,' Argon said. 'He should not take precedence over a bride.' He shrugged. 'However, I will not say any more. You look too tired. You will go to bed now and rest.'

'Oh, but...' she began.

'No arguments,' Argon dictated. 'How long is it since you slept?'

She thought of the long, hot sleepless night in Athens, and made a face. 'It was so hot in my hotel last night...'

'You see? You need sleep. No wonder you look like a wraith from Hades!'

Clyte returned. 'Your room is ready,' she said gently. 'I have put a tray in the room. If you are hungry you can eat a meal before you sleep, just a simple little meal of bread and cold lamb and fruit.'

'It is sleep she needs, not food,' Argon grunted. 'You women think too much of the stomach, not enough of the soul. Sleep heals many things.'

Clyte retorted, 'Lie down and sleep then, old man, and let foolish women manage things without you.'

Leonie laughed, and Clyte gave her an approving smile. 'That is better! You begin to look human. Come...'

She ate some of the food Clyte had prepared, not wishing to offend her after her kindness, then undressed and slid into bed. The room lay in cool shadow. The blinds were down, and a sea breeze rustled through the room. She watched the blue-black shadows moving on the bedroom wall and slowly felt herself slide into sleep.

In the morning she was able to face Argon without any of the dread she had felt on the previous day. She was relieved, all the same, when he asked no questions. She sat with him for an hour, reading the English newspapers to him, then when he fell asleep she went down and helped Clyte with preparing the lunch. Clyte talked to her in English, but began to teach her a little more Greek at her request.

'One day I would like to be able to speak it fluently. After all, it is my language as much as English is ...'

Clyte nodded vigorously. 'Good, that is good! Greek is a very beautiful language. So, you did not like Paris?'

The question took Leonie off guard, and she started and flushed. 'Paris? Why, yes, I did like it, very much. It's a lovely city.'

'Yet you left it very quickly,' Clyte pointed out.

'I felt useless in that empty flat,' Leonie said defensively. 'Paul has a cleaning woman who comes in every day, and there was nothing for me to do. I'm not used to doing nothing all day. I was bored.'

'Bored? On your honeymoon?'

'Oh, Clyte,' Leonie broke out. 'You know perfectly well that my marriage was arranged, it wasn't a love match. Don't pretend to believe that I was a happy bride.'

Clyte looked at her anxiously. 'What went wrong, Leonie? Was Paul unkind to you? I could have sworn that...' Her voice tailed off into silence.

'Paul was not unkind,' Leonie said flatly.

Clyte sighed. 'Well, we are finished now. Why don't you go down to the beach for a while?'

'If you're sure you don't need me?'

'I am sure,' Clyte insisted. 'Enjoy yourself.'

The beach was deserted, the golden sands virgin and untrodden, the waves curling on to them in white-flecked breakers. A few gulls wheeled and dived over the water. The blue sky stretched endlessly without a cloud.

Leonie lay down on a spread towel, staring at the sky for a few moments, then on an impulse got up and ran down into the waves. She swam strongly out to sea. It was exciting to breast the rolling waves and feel them carry her forward. She felt as if she could swim on for ever and never return to the world she had left behind. But after a while, with a sigh, she turned back and swam inshore again. Reluctant, however, to leave the beckoning depths, she dived down into the clear, sun-freckled water and tried to touch the bottom. White-sanded shelves threaded with dark green seaweed which brushed clingingly against her thighs as she moved, sending little swarms of tiny silvery fish darting nervously out of her way as her slender, half-naked body cleft their watery home. She could taste the salt on her lips, hear the thunder of the waves in her ears. In this remote watery world she was almost able to forget her problems.

Later she sunbathed until the salt dried on her body, relaxing with limp limbs under the spell of the sun and the sea.

Heavily content, she returned to the house. She had lunch with Argon. They ate fish salad and hot pitta, drank sweet strong Greek coffee cup after cup, talking idly about Comus and the people. Then Leonie left Argon to have another of his necessary, frequent naps. He was looking even older than when she had first met him. His illness was taking its toll, and she was glad she had come back to be with him. Even his close relationship with Clyte was not enough. He needed his own family around him.

In the afternoon she also took a brief nap on her bed behind closed shutters. The slumbrous heat of the day cast a spell over the whole island. Animals and birds sheltered from the heat. There were few sounds to be heard. No breath of wind stirred the olive trees. Even the sea seemed to be hushed.

As the shadows lengthened, everyone began to wake up. A dog began to bark somewhere. Birds called in the cypresses. Somewhere on the hills the sheep bells began to tinkle again and she heard the distant bleating of a goat. Leonie got up, washed and changed, then went down to help Clyte with dinner.

She ate the evening meal with Argon again, this time moussaka and salad, then they played chess together for an hour. Argon won. Very pleased with himself, he said goodnight to her, and she went up to her room to bed. She could not sleep so early, so she read for a while until she fell asleep.

This first day became the pattern for them all. Day succeeded day. Leonie swam and sunbathed, read and played chess and sat with Argon talking. She ate her meals and took her afternoon sleep. The hours ticked past in a summer haze of content.

She began to forget about Paul. At first she had thought of nothing else. He had haunted her, waking and sleeping, stalking in her dreams like the ghost of Hamlet's father. But gradually she made herself turn off. She drove his image away through sheer power of will.

They had heard nothing from him, and Argon and Clyte carefully never mentioned him.

Leonie had thought for a while that he would write or telephone, but gradually she realised that he meant to do neither. No doubt he was already setting their divorce on foot. Or would he wait until after Argon's death to do that? She no longer cared. Her sense of self-preservation made it necessary for her to switch off and forget him, and she did just that.

About a month after her arrival a thought occurred to her that froze the blood in her veins. She had begun to notice certain things which gradually assumed a terrifying significance.

Was it possible that she was going to have a child? She stared at herself in her mirror, her face suddenly white, her eyes standing out against her skin like dark pools.

What an irony of fate if that one night should have such consequences!

She began to count the days, to watch herself like a hawk for other signs. She dared not mention it to Clyte. Clyte would be bound to tell Argon, and Argon would undoubtedly write to Paul—and the last thing Leonie wanted was for Paul to find out. She did not want his pity or his enforced company. If he knew she was carrying his child he would feel bound to stay married to her, and such a marriage could only be embittered by resentment on both sides, which would not be good for their child.

So for the moment she kept the news to herself, deciding that there would be no outward sign to betray her for some months yet.

She needed confirmation, however, and knew that if she saw the island doctor the news would rapidly flash around the whole island.

She had to leave Comus—there was no other answer. She went to Argon and told him that she had to return to England for a while. 'Just a week or two. I'll come back very soon, I promise.'

Argon stared at her, frowning. 'Why is it so urgent?'

'My aunt is ill,' she lied. 'I rang her last night and she said she would like to see me.'

She had, in fact, rung her aunt in England, to ask if she might pay her a visit. Clyte had already informed Argon of the telephone call, so Argon was easily convinced. Grudgingly, he agreed that she should go.

Two days later Leonie was in England. She took a hotel room in London and made a private appointment to see a doctor in Harley Street, not wanting to alert her aunt to her condition any more than she wanted Argon to know.

The doctor was soon able to confirm her pregnancy, and gave her advice about her care of herself, prescribing iron tablets and vitamin tablets for the moment.

'You're very brown, Mrs Caprel, and you look healthy enough, but during pregnancy it's often the case that a young woman develops iron deficiency. You must take care of your diet. Drink plenty of milk, eat fresh vegetables and fruit, and avoid fatty foods...'

She listened, nodding, then hurried away to think alone in her hotel room. What was she to do? She could not leave Argon alone during these last months, yet once her condition was realised, Paul would soon be told and then she would have to face a terrible problem.

She sat staring at nothing for a long time, coming to no conclusion.

At last she decided she was hungry. The hotel dining-room was half full when she arrived, and she was shown to a pleasant table by the window, looking out over a tree-lined avenue.

It was the early evening. The sun was just sinking below the skyline, illuminating the London roofs with a fringe of crimson light. She ordered her meal and waited for the first course to arrive, idly playing with her cutlery.

'Good heavens! Leonie!'

The voice made her jump out of her skin. Pale and shivering, she looked round.

Jake Tennyson stood beside her, his expression almost as startled as her own.

CHAPTER NINE

'WHAT on earth are you doing in London? Is Paul with you?' Jake asked curiously.

'No,' she said quickly. 'No, I'm alone. I'm visiting a relative over here.'

Jake smiled. 'Then may I join you? I hate to eat alone, and it's a piece of exceptional good luck finding you here like this. I've often thought about you, Leonie, since I got back here from Paris.' He pulled back a chair and sat down facing her, his fingers laced together, staring at her over the top of his hands. 'You don't look well, somehow. Is something wrong? Although you're as brown as a berry you have a haggard look about you.'

She laughed. 'Women love to hear things like that! Thank you, Jake.'

He grinned. 'I'm sorry. Was that very rude of me? This new haunted look doesn't detract from your good looks, you know. It underlines them.'

Leonie flushed at the admiration in his eyes. 'Oh.' Her lashes fluttered down to make a curtain on her golden-brown cheeks.

Jake watched her, tracing the fine curve of cheek and throat, the faint blue stains beneath her eyes which betrayed some inner conflict, the tremor of her passionately shaped mouth.

'You've been in Greece lately, I gather?' he asked.

She looked up again, eyes widening. 'How did you know that?'

He shrugged. 'I have friends in Paris, remember. I hear all the gossip.'

'Of course.' She paused, then asked. 'How is George?'

'Doesn't Paul keep you in touch? George is very well, quite recovered from his illness. He and Diane have gone away to the Canary Islands for six months' holiday. Paul has been very busy getting George's affairs in shape. George intends to retire now, and his merchant bank has offered Paul a directorship in his place.' Jake watched her closely, his eyes narrowed. 'You seem to find all this surprising. Doesn't Paul write to you?'

She met his eyes bravely. 'I'm not very interested in business matters.

Jake grimaced faintly. 'I see. So what have you been doing with yourself since I last saw you? A lot of sunbathing, from the look of you.'

She smiled. 'I've been on Comus for weeks—as you guessed, sunbathing and swimming a lot of the time. It's very relaxing on the island.'

'You look tanned, but you certainly don't look very relaxed,' Jake told her.

Her eyes shifted uneasily. 'I'm worried, of course.'

'About what?' Jake leaned forward urgently, his eyes fixed on her face with great intensity.

'About Argon, my great-grandfather. He's dying. Didn't you know?'

Jake looked almost disappointed. 'I see. I'm very sorry to hear it. He's a fine old man.'

'Yes, I'm very fond of him. I've got fonder of him than ever during these last weeks. I hate to think ahead at the moment. The future looks too grim For more reasons than Jake could ever guess, she thought to herself.

'For a newly married couple you and Paul have a very casual attitude towards each other,' Jake said slowly. 'How long are you going to be in London'

'I'm going into the country tomorrow, to visit an aunt of mine,' she said.

'How are you getting there?'

'By train, I suppose.'

'Let me drive you,' Jake suggested.

'Oh, no,' she protested. 'I couldn't give you so much trouble, although it's very kind of you to offer.'

'It's neither kind nor troublesome,' he said flatly 'I want to see you tomorrow.'

She felt her cheeks flushing. 'Jake! Don't start that again. I thought...'

'Leonie, stop thinking for a little while,' Jake interrupted her hastily. 'Just let things drift for a time. It might take that haunted look out of your face. What harm can it do for me to drive you to visit your aunt?'

She hesitated, biting her lip. She had enough problems on her mind without Jake adding more.

He put a hand across the table to take one of hers 'Please, Leonie,' he murmured softly.

She shrugged helplessly. 'Very well.' She could not be bothered to argue any further.

The waiter hovered expectantly. Jake looked

round, his face triumphant, and clicked a finger and thumb. 'I'll order now,' he said.

They took their time over the meal, talking and laughing easily together. Jake had a fund of funny stories which brought a sparkle into Leonie's eyes and eased the lines of strain around her mouth and nose. By the time they were drinking their coffee, Leonie was feeling far more relaxed and cheerful.

'It's a pity to break this up so soon,' Jake said, as they left the table. 'There's dancing in the ballroom tonight. Will you come and dance for half an hour?'

'Oh, I really think I ought to get to bed,' she protested.

Jake took her elbow and steered her towards the sound of dance music. 'Nonsense! A little fun would do you the world of good.'

She laughed, 'You talk as if I were an invalid!'

'I think you're someone with a lot on her mind,' Jake said gently. 'I would like to see your face looking the way it did the first time I saw you. You didn't have that remote look then. You were flushed and pretty and slightly indignant at my silly mistake, and I envied Paul.'

The ballroom was not over-crowded. They found a small table in a corner and sat down for a short time until a new dance began, then they moved on to the floor and danced. Jake was a graceful, deft dancer, and Leonie found the experience very pleasant, moving in his arms to the restful swirl of the music. He did not talk much, his chin resting slightly against her hair, his hand softly holding her in the small of her back.

After a few dances she excused herself, however. 'I really must get some sleep. I'm very tired.'

He insisted on seeing her to her room. Outside her bedroom door he took her key and unlocked the room for her. She took back the key and smiled at him.

'Goodnight, Jake.'

He bent his head quickly, before she could move out of the way, and kissed her. Half dazed by the good wine they had drunk and the warm air of the ballroom, Leonie did not resist, standing like a good child with her face upturned to his. Jake murmured half groaningly against her mouth, his arms came up around her and he pulled her hard against him. The gentle, friendly kiss altered, becoming demanding and hungry, till Leonie was startled into realisation of what was happening. She pushed against him, pulling her face back.

Jake ler her go at once. Wryly, he looked down at her. 'I'm sorry, but I was tempted beyond my endurance. You're a very attractive creature, Leonie.

She frowned, biting her lip. 'Jake, look, I don't think we should see each other tomorrow, after all.

'No,' he said quickly. 'I promise to be good. It was only a moment's weakness. I'll pick you up tomorrow after breakfast.'

He was gone before she could argue. She closed her bedroom door and stood leaning against it staring into the dark. Jake's kiss had awoken passion in her, a passion not for Jake but for Paul, and she had to struggle bitterly against a longing for him.

Would she ever see him again?

She was up early next morning, packed and ready to leave as soon as she had had breakfast. With the clear light of morning she felt a clear realisation of the dangers of seeing much of Jake. That kiss had been a warning. Whatever he said, he was far too interested in her, and she was far too vulnerable at this moment. Her own unhappiness had weakened her.

She decided to take a train after all, leaving a message for Jake. But as she left the hotel she saw him waiting outside in his car, and her look of unguarded surprise brought a dry smile to his handsome face. He met her and took her case.

'I came early because I suspected you might try to run away,' he said. 'I was right, wasn't I?'

'Jake, I think I ought to go by train,' she said apologetically. 'If Paul got to know about this he would be furious.'

'How is he to know? He's in Paris and we're here,' said Jake lightly.

She sighed, 'I wish you'd listen to sense.'

He grinned at her. 'While I drive you can tell me all about your aunt.'

Leonie had to smile. 'What an obstinate man you are!'

'That's right,' he agreed. 'So you'd better do as you're told, my dear.'

The drive was a pleasant one, through some of the loveliest English countryside, and the warm weather made it an even more enjoyable experience. They stopped for lunch at midday at a roadside inn where they ate their meal in a sunlit garden under a striped umbrella while sparrows and blue tits hopped and flew around them begging for crumbs.

Laughing at Jake as he crumbled a roll and carefully rationed it out among the birds, Leonie felt suddenly for the first time for weeks that she was happy, and her surprise at this discovery alarmed her. What had Paul done to her? Only a few months ago she had often been happy. Now a momentary pleasure like this could take her off guard and amaze her. She had ceased to expect happiness; she had ceased to hope for it. This was all Paul's doing.

Bitterness flooded along her veins. For the second time in her life a handsome man had ruined her happiness.

Jake was watching her when she looked up. He put out a finger and touched her lashes gently. 'Tears? Why?'

A smile quivered along her mouth. 'I don't know ...'

'My dear,' he said with concern, 'I hate to see you like this. What the hell is going on between you and Paul?'

'We must go,' she said, rising.

Jake followed her, his hands in his pockets, a frown on his face. He drove the rest of the way in moody silence. When they reached her aunt's home, Jake stopped the car and leaned back, staring at nothing.

'We're here,' Leonie said with an attempt at light-

'Is your marriage a farce?' he asked abruptly, turning to look at her.

She flushed, then paled. 'I'm not answering questions like that, Jake.'

'You don't have to. I know the answer. Your eyes give you away, you know.' He took hold of her hands and held them tightly. 'Leonie, come to me. I think I love you. I think I could teach you to love me, and I wouldn't be as blind to your rare sweetness of character as Paul seems to be. I would make you happy. When you've divorced Paul we could marry, live here in England.'

She was on the point of tears. 'You're very kind, Jake. I'm deeply touched. But no, it's impossible...'

Then suddenly they both saw someone standing beside the car, watching them with a menacing scowl.

Leonie withdrew her hands from Jake's grasp, her face turning scarlet under Paul's accusing eyes. Jake sat immovably, staring at Paul, their eyes clashing.

Leonie scrambled out of the car and faced Paul. 'What are you doing here?'

'Strange as it may seem, looking for my wife,' he bit out. 'Argon rang to tell me you were coming here, and I arrived yesterday. You didn't show up.' His blue eyes flashed at Jake. 'I gather I may guess why.'

She did not reply, her eyes dropping nervously away from the anger in his glance.

Jake had got out of the car now. He moved towards Leonie, his face anxious. 'Don't look so frightened, my sweet. He shan't hurt you while I'm here...'

Paul lunged like a sleek golden tiger, his fist swinging at Jake's chin. The next moment Jake was flat on his back with an astonished expression. Leonie gave a gasp of horror.

'Paul, you shouldn't have done that!' She knelt beside Jake. 'Are you all right?'

Jake ignored her, rising to his feet, his hand rubbing his chin. 'You caught me off guard that time, you bastard! Just try and do it again.'

Paul's face was taut with anger. 'Get into the house, Leonie,' he said tightly. 'Tennyson, come round into the garden where we won't have so many witnesses.'

'No!' Leonie cried desperately. A wave of swimming heat rose inside her head. She felt as if she were drowning in the clear waters of the Aegean, the thundering of the waves in her ears, the taste of the salt on her lips.

Jake looked round in alarm as she swayed. He caught her as she fell, holding her gently against his body.

'Get away from her!' Paul snapped, snatching her out of Jake's arms.

'She's as white as a ghost,' Jake said anxiously.

'Go into the house and get them to ring for a doctor,' Paul ordered. 'I'll carry my wife indoors.'

For a moment the two men's eyes fought a duel over her limp body, then Jake reluctantly moved away.

Leonie recovered consciousness as Paul gently

laid her on a bed in one of her aunt's demure little bedrooms.

She lay, her lids fluttering weakly, staring at the ceiling. Paul stood watching her in moody silence, the sunlight gilding his butter-gold hair.

Her glance shifted to him. Her brows jerked together. 'Paul...' She remembered what had happened and tried to sit up. 'Jake? What happened? You didn't hurt him?'

'No, I didn't hurt your lover,' Paul bit out scathingly. 'You saved him when you fainted.'

She quivered. 'He isn't my lover...'

'Not yet? Never mind, it won't be long,' Paul said in a tone that made her feel sick.

There was a tap at the door, and a man came into the room. Leonie recognised him as her aunt's doctor. He smiled at her comfortingly. 'Well, my dear, how are you? Fainting, I hear? That can't be allowed, you know.' He glanced at Paul. 'She's only been married a few months, I understand. Is that the answer, I wonder?'

Paul's look of incomprehension was succeeded by a look of absolute amazement. He shot a narrow-eyed glance at Leonie, who was crimson and trembling against her pillow.

The doctor did not wait for a reply, bending to take her pulse, to look at her eyes and ask her a few discreet questions. Behind him Paul stood like a stone statue, watching her. Leonie could not meet the blue glare of his eyes.

'I think a few hours' rest should put matters to rights,' the doctor said. 'These things happen. No cause for alarm.' He patted her hand. 'If anything else happens, get in touch with me at once, though. We can't be too careful in the first months of a pregnancy. Rest and a light diet will put you to rights, eh?'

When he had gone, Paul moved over to the window, his back to her. 'He said a pregnancy?'

Weakly, she murmured. 'Yes.'

'You're pregnant?'

'Yes.'

Paul turned suddenly and faced her, his blue eyes bright and glittering. 'And you didn't tell me?'

'I...'

'You didn't think I had a right to know?'

'I didn't want to tell you,' she said miserably. 'It might have made you feel ... that you had to stay married to me...'

'You're damned right it makes me feel that,' he cried furiously. 'It is my child, isn't it?'

She went red. 'Of course it is!'

'How long did you think it would be before I found out? You couldn't keep it from me for long.'

'I thought by then you might have started divorce proceedings,' she mumbled.

'So that you could marry Jake?' he demanded.

'Jake?' She stared at him blankly. 'This is nothing to do with Jake. I thought you might want to marry Diane.'

Paul stiffened, staring at her intently. 'I see. That's why you stayed on Comus for weeks, never writing...'

'You didn't write to me,' she protested.

'I didn't vanish out of your life as you did out of mine,' Paul stated bitterly. 'I came back to the flat and you'd gone, without a word of where you'd gone to ... I rang the airport and found out you'd flown to Greece. I would have followed you, but that evening George had a relapse and I was torn between staying in case he died or flying to Greece to find you. I rang Argon, and he told me he thought you needed to be left alone for the time being. So I left you alone.' His blue eyes were like bright stones as he watched her. 'And I waited for you to write and ask me for a divorce.'

Her lashes stirred on her cheek. 'Would you have given me one?' she asked faintly.

'Like hell I would!' he snapped. 'I was just waiting to hear you ask so that I could have the pleasure of telling you precisely why I would never divorce you.'

Her lids lifted. The shadowed eyes looked at him. 'Tell me now.'

'This isn't the time or the place,' he said. 'You're too weak. It will have to wait.'

Leonie moved off the bed and stood beside it, her head swimming a little. 'There! You see? I'm perfectly all right now.'

Paul leapt across the room in a fury of anxiety. 'Lie down again, you little fool! Do you want to lose your baby?'

As he touched her, something deep inside her tightened to a pitch of unendurable sweetness. She drooped like a flower against him, her lids lowered to hide the expression in her eyes. Paul's arms came round her, he lifted her and swung her back on to the bed.

She looked up at him, trembling with the force of her passion for him, and their eyes met, their faces very close together as he lowered her against the pillows.

Paul made a sound deep in his throat, a groan of hungry desire which was unmistakable. 'Leonie,' he muttered thickly.

They moved together in one involuntary movement, their mouths meeting, clinging, parting. Paul's hands slid over her body, he flung himself down beside her on the bed and the long kiss deepened until her head swam and her breath hurt in her lungs.

Just as she thought she would faint again, he lifted his mouth and looked at her, smoothing back a stray lock of hair from her flushed forehead.

'Why did you never let me see it before?' he demanded with the bright triumph of the conqueror. 'Why did you keep me in suspense all these weeks?'

'I thought you loved Diane,' she murmured, half laughing, half sighing. 'How could I have guessed you loved me? You didn't want to marry me. You were furious when Argon suggested it.'

'Of course I was furious,' Paul said with an echo of that anger. 'I was already falling for you then—I started to fall the very first day, on the plane to Comus. You were so defiant yet so sweet. How could I help being attracted? Each time we saw each other I fell faster. Then Argon dropped his bombshell. I was humiliated by what he said in front of you, but to have a marriage suggested, when I was already thinking that marriage to a girl like you might not be so bad after all ... that rubbed my pride raw. I knew it would ruin everything if we married by arrangement.'

She remembered vividly her own contempt for him because he was prepared to accept such a marriage. 'Then why did you agree?' she asked in bewilderment.

Paul's mouth twisted sardonically. 'How could I not? Once Argon had made the suggestion, any attempt I made to get close to you would seem to you like a devious method of doing as Argon wanted. I couldn't have made love to you without you suspecting my motives. I was faced with no alternative. So I married you, hoping that in time we could grow closer. Why do you think I took you off to that shepherd's hut? I needed time alone with you, time to coax you into regarding me with less contempt.' He grinned at her. 'And then you sprained that damned ankle of yours and we had to leave.'

'You were so horrid in Paris,' she said reproachfully.

'My dear girl, I was terrified of Jake. I've known him for years. I know every expression on his face. I saw the way he looked at you, I saw the smile in your eyes as you looked at him.'

'You were jealous,' she murmured, her mouth dimpling.

He punched her chin. 'Yes, madam, I was as jealous as hell. Everything between us was so delicately balanced. I knew by then that you were warm and loving, capable of passion. I knew you were ready to fall in love.'

'Oh, did you?' she asked, raising her chin defiantly.

He grinned. 'Have you forgotten the way you behaved when you were tipsy? Believe me, I had a hard time that night. I was very tempted to make love to you.'

She looked at him through her lashes. 'As you did later?'

His face sobered. 'Do you hate me for what happened that night? I was driven by devils I couldn't control; jealous of Jake, afraid he would steal you away from me, longing to make love to you ... I thought that by forcing the situation I might somehow resolve it.' He grimaced. 'I suppose I was slightly drunk. I had a mad notion that once I'd made love to you, everything would be perfect, that you would realise you loved me and we would be happy ever after.'

'It could have been,' she whispered, her face pink. 'But next morning you were so different.'

'I was horrified by what I'd done, I was too much of a coward to face you, so I ran away...'

'Oh, Paul,' she half laughed, half sobbed. 'Paul, dearest...'

He bent his head and they kissed softly.

'But Diane,' she said, as they drew apart. 'You haven't said anything about her.'

He looked at her in astonishment. 'My dear girl, you can't have believed I was in love with Diane?

What on earth put that lunatic idea into your head? The woman is a monster! I've always been sorry for poor old George married to her, but for his sake I try to keep her happy. Of course, she likes to pretend that all George's friends are in love with her, but in fact none of us can bear the sight of her.'

Leonie was silent from sheer incredulity. They stared at each other, then Paul laughed aloud.

'Don't you believe me?'

'She's so beautiful!'

'So are tigresses, but no sane man gets into a cage with one!'

'Paul,' she sighed happily. 'Paul, we must get back to Greece at once...'

He stared at her in surprise. 'Why the hurry? The doctor said you must rest.'

'I want to see Argon's face when we tell him about the baby,' she said joyfully.

Paul smiled slowly. The sunlight from the window fell across his smooth golden head turning it into a halo of splendour above his handsome face. Leonie's eyes caressed him adoringly.

'Oh, Paul, I love you,' she whispered.

Paul's blue eyes blazed down at her. 'My darling girl!' A little grin twitched at his mouth. 'Poor old Jake, I can even be sorry for him now. I could have killed him when I saw you two roll up just now...' His eyes narrowed. 'Where were you last night, by the way?'

'In a London hotel,' she said demurely.

Paul's face tightened but he waited for her to go on.

'Alone,' she said, laughing.

'Don't tease me, Leonie,' Paul said thickly. 'I have a low threshold where jealousy of you is concerned, I'm afraid. So how did you meet up with Jake?'

'By accident,' she told him, going on to explain about the dinner on the previous evening, the dancing and her decision to leave without Jake. 'But when I got out of the hotel he was already there, so I had no choice but to let him drive me here.'

'Clever Jake, he would have guessed what you'd do. What was he saying to you when I came out? He was holding your hands, wasn't he?'

'He wanted me to leave you for him,' she admitted. 'I feel responsible for having encouraged him. I was unhappy and Jake was there ... I shouldn't have let him think I might ever turn to him.'

'Poor old Jake,' Paul nodded sympathetically. 'How easy it is to feel pity for the loser when you're the winner. It was a very different story when I was terrified that he might turn out to be the winner.'

'One day Jake will meet the right woman,' Leonie said wisely. 'He wants to love someone, and that's the first step towards loving.'

'When did you start loving me?' Paul asked, kissing her neck with a slow, hot insistence.

She put her hand up to his bright head. 'Long before I ever met you, I suspect,' she said, laughing. 'When I was a silly schoolgirl who kept a scrapbook filled with pictures of my handsome playboy cousin. I used to dream about meeting you.'

'You never told me that!'

'I would have died rather than admit it until now,' she said lightly. 'Then there you were on the plane to Greece, and you didn't recognise me...'

'What a fool I was!' he murmured wryly.

'Darling, let's go back to Comus tomorrow,' she said gently. 'We can start again there. Our second honeymoon...'

He raised himself on his elbow and looked down at her, at the black hair straying over the pillow and the passionate pink mouth, the shining eyes looking up at him. 'Yes,' he said deeply. 'The Master of Comus will take his bride home so that the whole island can rejoice over the news that a new heir is expected.'

'The Master of Comus...' she murmured. 'Argon said something about that.'

'It's the title given to the head of the family,' he explained. 'One day it will pass to our son.'

Her eyes were filled with dreams as she watched his face. 'Our son,' she murmured softly to herself. 'Oh, I'm so happy I'm afraid...'

'You need never be afraid again,' Paul said with certainty. 'I'm going to make you the happiest woman in the world.'

She laughed, her eyes filled with love and amusement. 'Oh, Paul, you're still the most arrogant, self-assured man I've ever met!'

'And you, my spitfire, are the most teasing, infuriating woman I've ever met ... and I adore you.'

She put her arms around his neck and pulled him down to her, her eyes closing in ecstatic surrender as their mouths met.

Harlequin
Announces the
COLLECTION
EDITIONS
OF 1978

Harlequin's Collection 12
ANDREA BLAKE
Night of the Hurricane

Harlequin's Collection 106   1.25
ANNE WEALE
If This Is Love

stories of special
beauty and significance

25 Beautiful stories of particular merit

In 1976 we introduced the first 100 Harlequin Collections — a selection of titles chosen from our best sellers of the past 20 years. This series, a trip down memory lane, proved how great romantic fiction can be timeless and appealing from generation to generation. Perhaps because the theme of love and romance is eternal, and, when placed in the hands of talented, creative, authors whose true gift lies in their ability to write from the heart, the stories reach a special level of brilliance that the passage of time cannot dim. Like a treasured heirloom, an antique of superb craftsmanship, a beautiful gift from someone loved, — these stories too, have a special significance that transcends the ordinary.

Here's your 1978 Harlequin Collection Editions . . .

More great Harlequin 1978 Collection Editions

122 Moon Over Africa
Pamela Kent
(#983)

124 Lady In Harley Street
Anne Vinton
(#985)

126 Will You Surrender?
Joyce Dingwell
(#1179)

123 Island In The Dawn
Averil Ives
(#984)

125 Play The Tune Softly
Amanda Doyle
(#1116)

Original Harlequin Romance numbers in brackets

ORDER FORM—Harlequin Reader Service

In U.S.A.:
MPO Box 707,
Niagara Falls, N.Y. 14302

In Canada:
649 Ontario St., Stratford,
Ontario N5A 6W2

Please send me the following Harlequin Collection novels. I am enclosing my check or money order for $1.25 for each novel ordered, plus 25¢ to cover postage and handling.

☐ 102	☐ 107	☐ 112	☐ 117	☐ 122
☐ 103	☐ 108	☐ 113	☐ 118	☐ 123
☐ 104	☐ 109	☐ 114	☐ 119	☐ 124
☐ 105	☐ 110	☐ 115	☐ 120	☐ 125
☐ 106	☐ 111	☐ 116	☐ 121	☐ 126

Number of novels checked ⸻@ $1.25 each = $ ⸻

N.Y. and N.J. residents add appropriate sales tax $ ⸻

Postage and handling $ ⸻.25

TOTAL $ ⸻

NAME ⸻
(Please print)

ADDRESS ⸻

CITY ⸻

STATE/PROV. ⸻ ZIP/POSTAL CODE ⸻

ROM 2181